◦⁓ꝏ⁓◦

WITCHY ILLUSIONS

A Novel

Stephen Spotte

Is it possible to have a false perception of an illusion?

Don DiLillo, *White Noise*

CHAPITRE UN

BEING DEAD HAS ITS ups and downs. On the upside you can stop worrying about death. The saying "you only live once" is easily flipped on its head because you only die once too, and the instant that moment arrives the memory of whether the experience was agonizing or serene no longer matters and never did. Why? Because the recollection of physical pain to the living exceeds memory's capabilities. Dredging up and replaying in the mind the exact feeling of a laugh or a bone snapping are equally impossible. You might recall the event, but reprising the actual sensation is impossible.

Such trivial issues then pale before the depressing scene all around, as you soon discover after stepping over the line separating the quick from the dead. Souls in uncountable numbers stumble here and there in differing states of disbelief and confusion, many not having fully realized their change in substantiality, others refusing to accept that death is even possible. Included among the former is the same contubernium of Roman soldiers in tight formation that routinely marches past me, eyes focused ahead, sandals kicking up clouds of spectral dust. Beside them a ghostly decanus barks the cadence in Vulgar Latin. They disappear into the mist in perfect formation only to return from the opposite direction. Of those refusing acceptance of their personal mortality are tattered wisps clawing at the windows of their former dwellings or pounding with a self-detached arm or leg on what once were their doors, wailing *"See me! See me!"* Their manic actions are for naught: the dead are invisible to the living, the latter deaf to their voices. For these solipsistic pilgrims eternity will seem exceptionally long.

And I? My name is Barthélemy de Chassenée, born in the year of our Lord 1480 at Issy-l'Evêque, Burgundy. I was in life an attorney noted for successfully defending the rats of Saône-et-Loire who ate the peasants' grain ripening in the fields and stored at the granary within the city walls of Autun. That tribunal occurred during the year of grace 1508 in Autun's ecclesiastical court. Later, I was advocate for Madame Truye, a sow accused of devouring a child in its bassinette on a farm outside this same city; still later I represented a putative werewolf, actually a harmless eccentric gone mad with rabies who terrified the citizens of Magny-Cours but did them no harm. I lost both cases in secular court, outcomes for all purposes preordained in these times that decree unequivocally mankind's exalted position in the hierarchy of earthly life, the only being created in God's image, making such a belief beyond reproach. The proceedings, however, were not without astonishing publicity that did much to burnish my reputation throughout central France, reaching even to Paris and substantially increasing my wealth.

Please excuse the momentary distraction, but a frantic soul is pounding on the door of his former house using a rotting leg torn from his own corpse and shouting at the inhabitants. Failing to elicit a response he now tries to force the latch. It will not budge. He moves to a window and peers in, shading his eyes with a hand. I move closer and look over his shoulder. He ignores me, perhaps unable to perceive my presence. Together we watch two children sitting on the bare wooden floor playing a desultory game involving sticks of different lengths. Nearby a woman, evidently their mother, sits on a man's lap. He reaches underneath her tunic and forces a hand between her legs causing her to squirm about. She throws back her head and laughs soundlessly, like an image in a painting. The children ignore them. My ghostly eavesdropper collapses into a sitting position and holds his head in his hands. He weeps. Eventually, he stands on his remaining leg and hops to another window of the same house. I follow, and together we peek inside. This room is inhabited by an old woman. She sits alone in a chair knitting with arthritic fingers, humpbacked and frail; her hair is gray, eyes cloudy with cataracts. A low fire flickers in the hearth. The man wails and scratches at the window. He wants to touch her. He pounds the glass with ghostly fists, making no impact. Unaware, she does not look up. His mother? No, his wife. The children and her lover, where are they? Grown, gone, perhaps dead. Life in these times is short for most, and mean. Eternity is unending, but earthly time zips by in a blink, a heartbeat. Between the first window and the second has passed a lifetime.

Humbert de Révigny, my adversary in court and always my friend, served as prosecutor in the three trials I mentioned. I learned early in the tribunal of the rats that Révigny had died several years before and taken up residence in Hades, that Satan occasionally furloughs him back among the living to participate in legal proceedings he finds amusing or threatening his hubris. Révigny once spoke openly to me about this unusual arrangement, his discourse ending with an ambivalent shrug as if to say, that's it, there's nothing more. He enjoys the high status as a member of Satan's inner circle, while complaining that the surroundings are deficient in some ways. He mutters repeatedly about the weak reading light, but most annoying is the constant noise and disruption, notably the shrieks of the damned burning at their fiery stakes mingling in chorus with those of the demons torturing them; this and the ceaseless din of construction as Satan's minions excavate new passageways through bedrock to accommodate an endless flood of immigrants from Purgatory. And, of course, the heat can be distressing. Hell evidently is about pain, heat, and distraction.

I shall say it straight out, then let the matter drop: Révigny appears to me as a green demon who always smells faintly of burning sulfur. His demonic form is tall and thin with slouching posture and eyes that change color depending on his level of excitement. When he's bored or merely idle they pulse in luminescent green, shifting to pale yellow if his mood is thoughtful, then to bright yellow when slightly aroused. When he becomes excited or angry the yellow flashes hot orange and at its peak a blinding red at which instant they glow like a pair of fiery coals. Perhaps most marvelous is what I call his "cocoon," a transparent and mostly impermeable membrane covering his entire body that moves and flows in synchrony with his own movements. Inside this device is a supply of burning brimstone, the fumes of which its inhabitant prefers to breathe instead of earthly air. This is, as I say, how I perceive Révigny. To the living his appearance is that of a bald, decrepit older man shuffling toward his end of days, avuncular, charming, and harmless. If only they knew!

Révigny, speaking as Satan's representative, had once offered me a seat in Hell's inner circle when my own end-time arrives. Realizing that Heaven was never an option I anticipated the experience with considerable curiosity, although at the moment I seem to be doing penance somewhere else, perhaps Purgatory. If so, the surroundings are nothing like the clerics describe. Where are the souls roasting in their personal fires that burn hot but never consume, of which Purgatory hints and Hell guarantees? And the demons dashing about tormenting everyone, where are they? I hear howling and sobbing; I hear and see anguish everywhere, although nothing that might signal physical pain. Perhaps this netherworld into which I fell at the instant of death is merely Purgatory's ante-room; maybe the worst is yet to come.

We can't see our feet for the gray, odorless fog swirling around our lower legs. It offers no resistance. Everyone seems to be standing knee-deep in it regardless of individual height, child and adult alike. Whatever the name of this milieu, we inmates appear trapped in an airy firmament. I sense nothing solid beneath me, but neither can I see a sky. Instead of a panorama the horizon vanishes into this endless mist where sounds are absorbed, sometimes returning as faint echoes: the remainder of a scream or a fragment of an agitated curse.

Occupants of this strange place, at least those near enough to observe, appear unaware of their predicament and of those around them. They act oddly incurious, self-absorbed, wandering aimlessly like discarnate barnyard fowl, each seeking something different, something necessary to fulfill a personal need or desire, all struggling toward an individual goal. No one seems fulfilled. My former senses lie dormant, unable to be aroused with any immediacy. I too wander in this perpetual mist out of touch with myself, although I seek nothing. What I see, hear, touch, smell, feel are delayed perceptions similar to dreams and snippets of memories. The state of "now" felt by the living, that vital moment in which life takes place and we exist, disappeared the instant I crossed over. Since then every thought and footstep, every gesture, seems to have occurred before, although somewhere else, not here. No, surely not here....

Once oriented I looked around for quill, ink, and paper then realized, to what purpose? What would I write, and who would read it? A ghostly pen dipped in ghostly ink; inconsequential words scratched on spectral paper could result only in ghostly sentences invisible to the living. How do you post a ghostly letter, and who could deliver it through the barrier? So, indeed there is no way of re-crossing the divide, no means of relaying a message. To the living a ghost and his spectral accoutrements truly are invisible, or I concluded until remembering that Révigny makes the crossing routinely in both directions. How strange that must be.

Without having realized it I died suddenly of

apoplexy during an erotic daydream in the midst of the werewolf trial, although only Révigny noticed. Everyone else thought I fainted and assumed the bailiff had aroused me by putting wet compresses on my forehead and eventually helping me to my feet. The end had come as I stood before the court delivering a heated rebuttal, all eyes watching. I fell dead in my lawyerly robe in the manner of a soldier dying in battle with sword in hand, a shepherd gripping his crook, a priest clutching his cross, a farmer whose gnarled fingers will not unclasp the hoe. All of us struck down by the reaper on life's individual fields of battle, each in his private instant of "now." Without being conscious of it the fatal blow had been struck on Tuesday the 2nd of October, the year of our Lord 1515.

My death followed a hiatus of unknown duration, at least to me. During the event I saw a blinding white light. As it attenuated and eventually vanished I too thought I had lost consciousness momentarily and recovered, but obviously not. After court adjourned for the day Révigny and I, as was our custom, went to the tavern of the inn where we lodged and sat at our usual table. I recall Révigny's depthless eyes modulating between vivid orange and fiery red. He was clearly distressed about something, alternately crossing and uncrossing his bony green legs and sighing, his forked serpentine tongue once flopping out and resting a moment on the table. After squirming about in his chair and gazing at the ceiling he looked directly at me and said, "Do you fear death, Barthélemy?"

"Less than disliking the prospect of absence from life," I said.

"Well put. Do you pray?"

"No. I don't think it's wise to draw God's attention. He's not likely to approve of what He sees or believe what He hears out of my mouth."

"Quite right. Probably just as well. I now have something important to tell you, but how to say it while minimizing the shock? Straight out, I suppose, so here it is: Monsieur Chassenée, you are dead."

"What?"

"You no longer kill time, so to speak, among the living. You have become a specter like me, a ghost. Death has struck you down, my friend. You have acted in your last play, at least as a living being. As the saying goes, *la farce est jouée.*"

"Oh, dear God!" I said.

"Révigny shook his head in mock sadness. "He can't help."

"Did you make certain I'd stopped breathing?"

"Of course, although in your case it was somewhat difficult. Often a feather is burned under an unresponsive patient's nose to determine whether he's dead or merely unconscious. Another test is to balance a dish of water on the patient's chest and watch for any ripples that might indicate breathing. You seem to have no neck or chest. Your stomach meets your chin, so where to set the dish where it wouldn't roll off? A candle can be held close to the patient's face and an eyelid pushed open. The pupil should contract if life remains. If the pupils differ in their response this indicates the individual is alive, perhaps suffering a concussion or an incidence of apoplexy. No, Barthélemy, you were dead at that instant and remain so."

"But others will be aware of my new status. How can they not notice the smell of decay? Who passes a corpse without seeing it?" When I remember this *repartie*, why were those my first thoughts?

Révigny leaned back in thought, the color of his eyes having diminished to pale yellow. "Will anyone notice your change of state? Yes and no. The living make all effort to avoid the dead and not think about them. People are selfish, and the status of others hardly matters. My own subterfuge has been honed well, and I pass with ease through the upper world as a living man. Not to worry, simply follow my example. We shall think of something when the occasion arises. Plague of many sorts sequesters in everyone's exhalations and exudations, in each person's blood and spirit, unseen although the effects are apparent to all. I had arranged with Satan a while ago that when your moment came we would keep you chugging along, so to speak, as if nothing happened except a fainting spell. And so, the werewolf trial continued except for that brief disruption, business as usual. It ended without anyone noticing you had died, including you." He grinned, displaying his green teeth and gums. "Now erase that grim look. We have an upcoming witch trial, remember? It promises to be great fun. Good times are ahead!"

"I hope so," I said, becoming contemplative. Had I been a good person in life? Hardly. I disparaged my wife, although mostly in self-defense. I had been an adulterer, scourged my serfs, and routinely took the Lord's name in vain. I attended Mass only when falsely misrepresenting myself to clients as a man of piety and honesty, then later stole from them after gaining their trust. I lied to everyone when it was in my interest, including judges and the clergy, and blithely tiptoed around the edges of justice to get clients guilty of terrible crimes exonerated and in so doing line my own pockets with their ill-gotten *sous*.

And this is only the beginning. In short, I had committed all the seven deadly sins—pride, envy, gluttony, avarice, wrath, lust, and sloth—some repeatedly and many eagerly. Of the seven Christian virtues listed by Aquinas—prudence, justice, temperance, courage, faith, hope, and charity—I measured up to none. Clearly, I deserved to spend eternity in Hell and fully expected to, but when Révigny suggested that terms of the sentence might be negotiable with Satan I said to myself, why not? Of course, why should I trust Révigny, in his heyday among the most dishonest lawyers in all France? Once again, why not? What had I to lose?

I tried to recall an instant during that brief interlude, or twilight period, when my demise might have become obvious. How could I have forgotten such an important moment, standing as I now did somewhere in the netherworld? Then our conversation in the tavern began forming in memory. Révigny had looked at me and said, "When was the last time you shit, Barthélemy?"

The question was startling, seeming so out of context. "I have no memory of the last time," I said.

Révigny then stood—and this moment I well remember. He looked around the tavern shaking his fist and yelled, *"You must examine your turds, people, or notice their absence! Therein lies the proof of life and death!"* A fistfight had broken out, and in the escalating *mêlée* no one noticed. The room filled with shouts and catcalls encouraging the two combatants, who were nearly too drunk to stand. Wagers were being made, and the patrons were shifting tables and chairs, clearing space for a makeshift arena.

Following his outburst Révigny sat and stared at me. "Think back to our conversations over the years about demonology. Although not a demon, you are a ghost, and this amounts to nearly the same thing." I had to lean forward to hear. "Nobody shits in the afterlife, *mon amie*. When allowed furloughs back on Earth we privileged denizens of Hades eat and taste food but don't digest and excrete; we drink alcohol with the living without becoming inebriated. Hangovers after nights of debauchery are unknown to us, which sounds almost heavenly until realizing that by not getting drunk neither are you experiencing the joy of making a fool of yourself."

CHAPITRE DEUX

WE DRANK FAR INTO the night discussing many things, and in the morning I was puzzled to awake at the hour of prime with a clear head. The day was devoted to packing, settling accounts with the innkeeper, and acquiring a few supplies for the trip. The trial was to be held at Bourges approximately seventy-five kilometers northwest of our present location in the town of Magny-Cours, site of the recent werewolf trial. I estimated a two-day ride for my retinue, assuming no unforeseen delays. Perhaps the road would be muddy and unpleasant or poorly marked. There could be questionable detours down narrow paths or through forests with lurking highwaymen. I had never traveled the route and hoped to find an inn with a tavern along the way where we could safely obtain food, drink, and suitable lodging for a night. However, we were prepared to sleep under the stars if the weather remained fair. The quality of the inns and taverns of modern France is variable. Some are respectable, others double as brothels and gambling establishments where the patrons not only eat, drink, and sing, but occasionally fight and kill one another. The trial could not begin until Révigny and I arrived, found a suitable inn, learned our way through the streets, and reviewed the case files. There was no particular rush.

My men and I departed Magny-Cours at the hour of prime on the following day, Wednesday October 17th, year of grace 1515. I had invited Révigny to join me on the journey to Bourges where he was scheduled to prosecute a young woman accused of witchcraft and I to defend her, but he declined, saying he had tasks elsewhere and planned to meet me at whatever inn I had chosen for the duration of the proceeding. Being a demon with supernatural powers, he could find us easily. We therefore parted company, and Révigny returned alone to Autun.

My contingent comprised two footmen, François and his son Alvin, who sat double on the mule, my servant Jamet on the donkey, and I riding the palfrey. My footmen are cowardly, inept, and essentially useless. However, as lifelong members of my estate I feel responsible for keeping them fed and housed despite how they try my patience. Doing so seems a matter of *noblesse oblige*.

François is insolent and obdurate in his patient way. Anyone meeting him would initially think him capable of planning and scheming until realizing the true depth of his mental deficiency, a classic example of how appearances can deceive. His eyes, which look in different directions, are unnerving, the "wandering eye" historically having been taken as evidence of a sly, duplicitous nature. François lacks the intelligence to meet even this low requirement. Still, he does his dissolute best. Alvin, now into his second decade, was born an imbecile and considers himself a bird, devoting hours to twirling in circles, arms outstretched and shouting, *"Je suis un oiseau! Regar de moi voler!"*

The road to Bourges was populated with the expected mélange of travelers. We encountered farm wagons, gypsy caravans, and an occasional coach bearing someone of the nobility, but most travelers were on foot: peasants, soldiers, peddlers, monks, tinkers, entertainers, beggars, orphans, and lepers, these last slumped at the roadside looking like piles of discarded clothing. As a dead man destined for Hell and hardly obliged to dispense charity I nonetheless felt pity for these poor souls and often dropped a bite of leftover food or small coin to the most pitiable. God graced mankind with dexterous hands to guide a pen, perform intricate surgery, play stringed instruments, yet the hands of these poor souls have been reduced to fingerless trowels and buckets, one to scrape the prize into the palm of the other.

Outside the towns and villages peasants and tradesmen had set up makeshift stands and even shops, the former selling mainly produce and cheap homemade items such as baskets, the latter available to mend clothing and shoes, saddles and harnesses, wagon wheels. . . .Everything is repaired or recycled and rarely discarded in these frugal times. We stopped once on the first day to stretch our legs and buy fruits and vegetables, bread, cheese, and sausages to eat as we rode or to pack away until supper and the next morning's breakfast if the night was to be spent in the open. The men were eating well and in good spirits, appearing to enjoy the sights.

Shortly after nones we abandoned the road for a deserted field beside a stream and hobbled the animals where they could drink and graze through the night. Jamet sent François and Alvin to gather enough firewood to burn until morning while he unpacked and made camp, although not before settling me comfortably at the foot of a large oak with a cup of wine and a blanket over my lap. The late afternoon was turning chilly. I had engaged Jamet as my servant while on the road to Magny-Cours just prior to the werewolf trial. He is an educated man, a former priest defrocked by his bishop for carnal knowledge of a married woman of his parish. He was a wandering beggar when first we met, but immediately proved more alert, trustworthy, and useful than my two so-called footmen ever had been despite their years of service.

The plan was to camp that night, the air being clear and calm. Sleeping rough has its good and bad aspects. To the good it saves the cost of room and board for myself and my men and animals. The animals can graze and drink for free, and we can enjoy a hearty meal and a night's sleep without being bothered by rodents, fleas, and bedbugs. I particularly dislike sharing beds with strangers, a necessary inconvenience when staying at inns, and being awakened in the middle of the night by soliciting whores and thieves poking through my belongings under pretense of begging.

On the negative side are the discomforts: lying on the hard earth, cold nights, and sometimes rain. However, we had brought adequate clothing and blankets, and the men would keep a warm fire burning until the hour of prime. Also to the negative we were unarmed, and bands of thieves and highwaymen are an ever-present danger.

Demons, goblins, and other supernatural beings, said to lurk everywhere in the countryside, are greatly feared even by the educated, especially after nightfall. As a dead man I wasn't bothered. What harm can one spirit inflict on another? In life I had never been especially superstitious or afraid of the dark, but being dead was still a new experience, and I fully expected that supernatural beings—perhaps I should say *other* supernatural beings—might become more apparent to me. Révigny had hinted as much, and even before dying I had been able to perceive the green eyeshine of forest hobgoblins as they raced through patches of moonlight, and hear their rustling in the underbrush. This experience had occurred in a haunted forest through which we passed on the road to Magny-Cours where I met Jamet. Oddly, Jamet could see these hobgoblins too. He was living in the forest at the time and remarked that they made terrible companions having, as he put it, the intellect of squirrels. So far, so good. This was a night of a nearly full moon that threw its rays deep into the shadows, offering the men some comfort. We supped on bread, cheese, and sausage, and I allotted each man a measure of wine, although not enough to dull our senses if we should be attacked in the night.

I awoke shortly after prime to propitious signs of fair weather. Jamet had set François and Alvin to unhobbling the animals. He handed me a cup of hot tea and a small loaf split lengthwise and toasted over the remaining coals. The men had already breakfasted, and Jamet then saw to packing and loading our belongings. We dawdled until near terce then mounted and again joined with the road west.

The day quickly became unseasonably warm, and despite the falling leaves and other signs of autumn the sun on our backs was hot. Near sext, as I was considering halting for a short rest in the shade, we heard a horse snort and turned in unison to look back at who might be gaining on us. It could have been anyone, considering our ambling pace.

They were three ragged knights newly arrived in France from the Crusades, or so they said. But how could that be possible in this day and age? They seemed anachronistic and decrepit in the extreme. Knights were near-mythic figures admired by all schoolboys in my youth. Everyone knew tales of their bravery, chivalry, and wealth. A knight was handsome and rode a fine charger. He might wear a mantle of ermine, a tapered tunic perhaps woven in some exotic eastern city like Constantinople, and tailored, form-fitting silk breeches. He would have on a doublet with a hauberk underneath, a shining helmet adorning his head, and for his arsenal a sword, shield, and lance. Attending him would be his heralds and pages. Prizes from jousting were the currency, coins still being rare in those years. In their place were pledges, horses and arms, land, and livestock. Often the losers were "enslaved" metaphorically, relinquishing their possessions temporarily to the winners and forced to "ransom" themselves in the name of the sport. To celebrate victories the winners held expensive banquets for their heralds and compatriots, laughing in the face of gluttony, even committing lust indirectly by wearing scarves, the gifts of female admirers. A successful knight might dine on foods suited to his status: in addition to bread and wine it was common for the menu to boast cranes, wild geese, and peafowl, roasted and served with pepper sauce.

But the three knights now coming toward us? One held a tattered piebald banner faded by years of sun and elements. The others bore rusted halberds, the axe edges chipped and dulled and the spikes broken in half. Despite the heat they wore full armor over what once had been brown tunics but now were rags. What scraps of shoulder fabric remained were decorated with barely discernible Maltese crosses. From their belts hung *aumônières sarrasines*, the silk purses carried by crusading knights to hold alms collected along the way to the Holy Land. Theirs were clearly empty. Of the men themselves their faces, hollow-eyed and skeletal, were barely visible inside their helmets, the countenances of corpses long abandoned to the desiccating desert wind. From the interstices of their armor came a stench of ancient flesh neither long absolved of death nor teetering on its edge, but somewhere between.

Their armor was ancient, so old I was overcome with astonishment. No one had seen such relics for centuries. It creaked and groaned audibly as the riders approached, decrying the combined ravages of age, rust, and misalignment of moving parts. Probably no tinker had ever been summoned to make repairs and properly lubricate the joints. One man's brassard and gauntlet were so dented it was a wonder he could extract his arm, assuming he ever did. These and other coverings had ceased to function as metal accoutrements and instead metamorphosed into such jointed carapaces as crabs and beetles wear. On another man the cuisse of the right leg was creased, undoubtedly to the point of causing pain; the greave of the left leg had split along the shinbone, and out of it oozed a dark, thick substance. The cuirass and both pauldrons of the third knight were heavily dented as if he had been beaten repeatedly with maces. All wore their swords scabbarded on the right, pommels hidden beneath gauntleted hands.

Their dusty war horses had once been fully armored, but now only isolated pieces of metal remained. One mount retained neither the flexible crinet with its jointed plates nor the chaffron, and all their cruppers had dissolved into history. A single horse had just its peytral, the other two nothing except their flanchards, but all three beasts appeared so frail that the added weight of a fly might bring them to their knees. They were stumbling and near failing, scarcely able to keep their heads erect, yet they plodded ahead on mandered legs, dull hides draped loosely over barely articulated bones at risk of punching through. As to their colors one was white, another bay tending toward reddish, and the third was black.

I engaged the men in conversation and began by asking where they had acquired their antique armor and weapons. They looked at each other and then at me without expression, their eyes dark holes.

"What do you mean, good sir?" said the knight sitting the white horse.

"Warriors outfitted as you haven't been seen in three centuries. Where have you been, and where are you going?"

"We are four knights recently returned from our Crusade in the Holy Land and on the way to Normandy, our ancestral homeland. The places in the east where Jesus walked have now been restored to

Christians everywhere. After visiting relatives we shall travel to Paris and pay respects to King Philip II. We suffer from the scrofula and were told that the king's touch will cure it."

I was stunned. The man's accent was indeed northern but strangely dated, and so was this mission he had just described. "King Philip died in the year of grace 1223," I said. I spoke the words carefully in a matter-of-fact tone, still undecided if these putative knights were simple-minded wanderers, dangerously insane, or fugitives from a traveling circus. "It's now the year of grace 1515. Please tell me your story, good sirs."

None of the men spoke on hearing this news, nor did their stoic countenances register surprise. "We awoke this morning in yon *boschage*," the knight on the red horse finally said, turning slowly in his saddle and pointing toward a mix of woodland and meadow from where they had come and using the archaic Old Norman term for such places instead of the modern *bocage*. "The landscape seemed at once strange and familiar. Strange because we had lain down to sleep at an oasis in the Egyptian desert last evening at sunset after watering and hobbling our horses. Familiar because when we awoke this morning the surroundings looked much like France and nothing like Egypt, or so we thought."

"That is because this *is* France," I said.

"But such a thing could not be possible," said the knight on the black horse, speaking for the first time.

"You're traveling a road that leads eventually to Normandy," I said, "although from this location you have a long way to go. There are inns, of course, so there won't be any need to sleep on the ground." That was when I heard the clatter of hooves behind me and turned to see François and Alvin attempting to drive my sluggish mule into a gallop in the direction from which we had come. But the mule only shifted into an awkward canter despite the kicks to its ribs and threats shouted in its ears by François. It was a clownish scene, the mule's stumbling gait and François and Alvin bouncing asynchronously on its back. The donkey, however, was stationary, Jamet having slid off and crawled under its belly from where he was praying loudly.

"Stop this nonsense and stand up!" I said.

Jamet obeyed at once. He brushed the dust from his clothes and said, "I apologize, Master. Blame it on my priest's training. I always feared the Apocalypse, and these knights seem eerily similar to the Four Horsemen described by Saint John in his *Book of Revelation*, but of course that's impossible because there are only three. I must be imagining War on the red horse, Famine on the black, and Pestilence astride his white steed. But if these are indeed the fabled Horsemen, where is Death riding his pale horse?"

There was momentary silence, then the rider of the black mount spoke: "Oh, he died too, but he must be around somewhere." He stood erect in the saddle and scanned the horizon, shading his eyes with a hand.

"He will appear soon," said the rider of the red horse. "Death never ventures far. You may be assured he's somewhere nearby."

Jamet, having heard enough, stumbled backward, dropped to his hands and knees, and scrambled back underneath the donkey.

The knight on the white horse raised an eyebrow.

"Your squire, sir?" A surprising question considering I looked nothing like a knight and wasn't even dressed as a nobleman. I shook my head.

"Then he is your page," said the knight on the black horse. The three of them patiently sat their broken mounts awaiting my answer.

"I suppose my servant would be more accurate," I said.

"And the two who ran away? Are they your pages?" said the rider of the white horse.

"Not quite. All three lack any redeeming qualities squires and pages might have, as you saw by how quickly they desert me at even the hint of danger, and my servant relied on prayer and hiding beneath an ass in the hope of saving his own."

"But we mean you no harm," the knight on the black horse said. "Our fighting days are through, having discharged our duties to God and country."

"We've been away many years, and our families must be anxious for our return," the knight on the white horse said. He sighed as if overcome by extreme fatigue. "*Contemptus mundi* is seen in the shortness of life and its evils," he said sadly. "From the child's first wail through subsequent tears, pain, suffering, illness, and the final exhalations of death. Fleas and lice plague us, our loved ones suffer and die; no one is happy. . . ever."

"When did you leave France for Jerusalem?" I said.

"It was spring in the year of grace 1212," said the knight on the white horse, "when thousands of us heard the call of Stephen of Cloyes, a shepherd boy of twelve years just like us. He was recruiting youths throughout France to join his Children's Crusade. The excitement was irresistible. We dropped our crooks leaving the sheep prey to the wolves and joined the throngs marching south. We three met on the road and became friends. It was not long before evil men joined the throng and like wolves began to prey on us as if we were sheep. When we reached Marseille the fairest among us, the blonde and blue-eyed boys and girls, were quickly separated from the masses of children and sold to Arab slave traders. They ended up in Tunis, Casablanca, Cairo, and other such places on the northern African coast as toys for wealthy noblemen and merchants. We three were swarthy and dark; the slavers never gave us a second look. Our dirt could not be washed away because it was part of us."

The knight on the red horse now spoke. "You say three centuries have passed since we bedded down in the Egyptian desert? But that seemed only last night! What became of the passing time? What you say must be true from the dress and speech of the people." He shook his head sadly. "With every war there are refugees. Those displaced are rendered mute, yet each has a story to tell."

"We have wandered long and far," said the knight on the black horse. "Not so unusual. Frenchmen returning from the Crusades occasionally detour through other countries, one being Abyssinia. We have on good authority, other travelers having reported it to us along the way, that the potters and blacksmiths of that strange land are able to change themselves into hyenas, and their guilds are greatly feared because of it. These trades are inherited, and in human form the men are recognizable by hairy bodies, eyes that gleam red, and harsh nasal voices. At night they metamorphose into ferocious maneaters. People tremble in their houses when the hyenas begin their nocturnal choruses of howls and demented laughter, and no one dares go out until the sun is high. Anyone coming across a fresh hyena carcass must immediately plug the anus or be liable to uninterrupted mirth, a sign of his own impending death. As a result of these fears the Church has excommunicated all potters and blacksmiths in that evil land, suspecting them of sorcery and consorting with witches and demons, but they don't care. They wear an earring in one ear as a badge of honor demonstrating loyalty to their fellows. Hunters occasionally kill a hyena on the vast plains with a ring in its ear.

"Other travelers we met passing through Abyssinia told us that witches there ride hyenas, and the hyenas themselves are incarnations of demons. In one form of the beast, the spotted variety, females have an elongated clitoris similar to a penis, making them almost indistinguishable from the males. Because of their androgynous state the females can have sex with each other, as well as with males, and with the bisexual moon." He slumped forward, evidently exhausted by his lengthy soliloquy.

CHAPITRE TROIS

"WE'VE SEEN MUCH, PERHAPS too much," said the knight on the black horse.

"Yes," said his comrade seated on the red horse. "What my companion says is true. Before *la peste noir* was the Great Famine that lasted from the year of grace 1315 to 1322. In 1337 the Hundred Years War began, which went on intermittently until 1453. In Cathay snakes, toads, and pestilential worms rained from the sky. So thick were their numbers that no one could see the sun. In India the earth shook and the sky hurled down stones and torrents of boiling blood. Surely the Apocalypse was just over the horizon. We believed we had seen such events, but how could that be possible?" His voice trailed off in confusion.

The knight mounted on the black horse now spoke again. "From Sicily came a report that a black dog holding a sword in its paw invaded a procession of citizens attempting to drive away *la peste noir*. And in 1349, at the height of its onslaught when the numbers of dead exceeded those of the living, rumors from Rome announced arrival of the Antichrist, destined to rule briefly until Last Judgment when the world ends. The Antichrist, so the prophets said, would bring peace and plenty, and a race of headless men would arise mysteriously and walk in peace among the rest."

The knight on the white horse leaned both hands on his pommel. "*La peste noire* was thought to have originated in Kyrgyz, or perhaps Crimea. Some believed it was spread by evil persons. Consequently, those who looked or acted suspiciously or seen as strangers were stoned in the streets or thrown into prison and sentenced to death by the courts. The clergy was pressured into staging processions during which any holy relicts housed in the local churches were included, and holy water was sprinkled here and there. No one realized that such gatherings merely hastened the spread of the disease. Children died in large numbers, many directly from *la peste noire*, others as an indirect result, their parents or other caregivers having succumbed and left them orphaned and unable to fend for themselves. In the absence of gravediggers, criminals and derelicts were hired for the grisly chore, and they committed many thefts. Crimes of all sorts became rampant. People mourned and lamented the dead and dying during the plague's early days but later became hardened, realizing they or their closest kin could be next.

"My comrades and I were still on Crusade in the East when *la peste noir* struck like a thunderbolt. That was the year of grace 1348. We thought the end of time had come. Knights toppled dead from their mounts as if impaled by invisible arrows, their faithful heralds and pages falling beside them. More than once we numbered too few to take the field, drawing comfort only in knowing that the unbelievers were suffering the same fate, that God seemed strangely impartial, intent on punishing both sides. Christian looked warily at Christian, fearful that anyone encountered on the road could be a *semeur de peste*. And truly, like grain *la peste noire* surely is sown, in this instance counting on the wind do its insidious work. Yes, *La peste noire*, or *la détempre* as some call it, is carried on the wind through effluvia from a sick person's breath, sweat, suppurating sores, even clothing. Contagions are without doubt windblown. Some people's eyes even emit miasmas or fluids containing the pestilence, and these too are picked up by the breezes. The actual carriers and instigators of death are tiny, invisible *semina*. Their effect is to start the victim's blood fermenting while agitating the spirit. Healers and theologians believed that if somehow made visible these tiny *semina* would appear as living, writhing monsters perhaps resembling dragons, serpents, and demons of various sorts.

"Pest-houses everywhere in that dubious place and time filled quickly to capacity and overflowed. They were too few to tend even a fraction of the sick. In the night death-carts passed through the streets ringing bells, just as in Europe, alerting citizens to bring out their deceased. We heard of many victims, especially those of weak constitution, literally dying of fright. Coffins were not to be had at any cost. Cemeteries were soon left with no consecrated ground. Then great pits were dug and the bodies hurled into them, Christian and Muslim alike, souls of the saved and the damned mingling in anguished confusion. Many afflicted with *la détempre* and knowing death was imminent crawled and limped to the death-pits and jumped in, some naked, others fully clothed or wrapped in blankets or rugs. Unknown numbers succumbed from suffocation and not *la peste noire* when the death-carts were emptied on top of them. Laborers at these communal burial pits, frequently ill themselves, alternately layered the dead with a covering of soil, filling the top two meters with compacted earth to discourage disinterment by dogs and wolves. As I said, *La détempre* struck without prejudice, striking down poor and rich, believer and infidel. The calamity visited all.

"It was told that some of the sick sought personal enemies and even strangers above their own estates whose wealth they envied and purposely touched them or breathed in their faces so they too would die. Others, not knowing they were ill and showing no signs, circulated with the healthy, thereby infecting them unintentionally with the invisible *semina*. These individuals representing death still walking were the most dangerous to society and difficult to avoid because they couldn't be recognized as insipient killers. Any gathering risked spreading *la détempre*, so traditional funerals ceased. People were unable to mourn their dead or follow them to the cemetery in procession; no church bells tolled, in part because there was no one to ring them. Of course, many died during this epidemic of other maladies too, such as consumption and grippe, but nothing like *la peste noire* had occurred since Noah's Flood erased all except a remnant of humanity from the face of the Earth.

"Most healthy persons wisely isolated themselves inside their houses, but others, thinking they were immune to *la peste noire*, carried on life as usual, mixing in the marketplaces, attending religious services, and frequenting shops and taverns, not caring that they might infect others and certainly not worried about themselves. This is one reason the malady could not be contained. Furthermore, few ever knew how or when they became infected. Oddly, conjurers, fortune-tellers, astrologers, and other such charlatans quietly disappeared, many no doubt surviving but not returning even when the epidemic abated. Many years passed before another gullible generation arose and welcomed back their kind.

"There were no cures, as everyone knows, and the best preventive was to flee to an uncontaminated place and hope you departed before the *semina* found and invaded you. The majority waited too long; consequently, the suburbs and countryside were quickly inundated as *la peste noire*, like an invisible swarm, fanned out from the city centers. People took to covering their noses and mouths with cloths soaked in perfumes, smelling salts, alcohol, and other aromatic substances. One popular means of trying to keep *la peste noire* at bay was to burn pitch or brimstone before open windows around the clock. Doing so was believed to kill or repel the *semina* before they could enter the dwelling and seek victims.

"As to longevity of the sick, their demise ordinarily was quick, most victims dying soon after appearance of the diagnostic buboes in the neck, groin, or armpits. The pain and torment of those who suffered longer were excruciating. You heard their screams from all directions, often joined in chorus by shrieks and shouts of neighbors suffering equally and awaiting our comrade Death's cold hand to touch them. Others feeling his icy breath on their faces wandered the streets weeping, wringing their hands, praying through futile sobs for God's mercy and generally lamenting their inevitable fate. The dying sometimes became delirious, singing and dancing in public, then dropping dead where they stood.

"If the pus- and blood-filled buboes were lanced the afflicted person sometimes survived. An alternative remedy was to douse these areas with strong caustics, causing the patient intense pain. Other symptoms of *la peste noire* include blackened fingertips, headache, vomiting, back pain, fainting, and fever. Some presented with only one or two of these signs accompanied by little or no pain, yet succumbed anyway.

"Ships coming from foreign ports, quarantined and forbidden to unload their cargoes, stood for weeks at anchor. On learning that *la détempre* was declining, people rushed into the streets and resumed life as before. Fools. Soon the slaughter commenced again. Most of these citizens believed that the bad air above and around them had by some miracle been restored to original purity, that now the contagion could not be caught from someone sick with it, that they were finally safe."

"You told me at first that you were four," I said.

"We were bewitched," said a new voice. I turned toward it and saw within arm's length a fourth knight no different from the others except that his ragged tunic had once been white. This and his horse, which was the palest gray with a strange, almost greenish cast. He had appeared soundlessly and looked at me with an empty stare so disturbing that I glanced away.

"Bewitched by whom?" I was curious, but also nervous. I looked at my hands holding the reins and tried to stop them from shaking. For what reason? I was now dead and thus immune to its consequences.

"By the angel Michael, God's holy warrior," said this new knight. "He touched us in the desert while we slept. The Lord has chosen us to carry out his holiest of missions, of which I am forbidden to speak except to say we're harbingers destined to wander until the end of time. The centuries are meaningless, mere wisps of ash in the wind. We won't be stopping to pay respect to the king. Our sole master is the Almighty; we bow to no one else. Our orders are to wait patiently until summoned for the final mission."

"And what will that be?" I said.

"It isn't my place to tell."

Then I understood. Jamet had been right. The fourth rider of the Apocalypse is Death, more powerful than his companions War, Famine, and Pestilence because he envelops their functions, using their weapons to serve his end. When not painted as a human skeleton Death is represented as a bearded man usually wearing a turban, although he sometimes sports a pointed hat or covers himself in a hooded cloak. He sits erect and expressionless astride a pale horse and holds in his hand a sword or a fiery brazier. Dragged behind in a harness tethered to the horse is Hades personified as a monstrous head, gaping mouth overflowing with agonized souls alight with the flames that burn hot but never consume. Among those depicted in their agony are kings, bishops, and monks, the most powerful agents of man and God. The lesson is clear: Death triumphs; he defies all and spares no one. It's Death who rides the pale horse.

"I now speak only to you," he said. "Your servant will be deaf to my words."

"And your companions? What about the ears of your fellow knights?"

"They know but remain confused about their own mortal status despite having experienced death. Some take longer than others to accept it."

"I understand, being no less confused," I said.

Death gave me a penetrating look. "Know that when the horn sounds at eternity's end you will not answer it."

"I know," I said. "We must be on our way. As you can see, my two cowardly footmen have returned on my now lathered mule, tails between their legs."

"Good day to you," said the knight called Death.

"And to you, sir. Will you continue on to Normandy?"

"Why not? We have nowhere to go and nothing to do until the end of time."

Chapitre quatre

WE ARRIVED WITHIN SIGHT of our destination the following day around nones. Bourges is situated in the Centre-Val-de-Loir at the confluence of the rivers Auron and Yèvre, although lesser rivers and streams also flow through the immediate area. We approached the city's outskirts from the east, slogging through the marshes of La Voiselle and eventually joining the queue at a ford where we crossed the river Voiselle itself, low now in the autumn dry season.

Once inside the city proper we stopped a priest, and I asked for recommendations and directions to a decent inn with a tavern. He hesitated before suggesting an establishment on rue Parerie very near the Avaricum district. It's called, he said, Atelier de Satan. Satan's Workshop! How appropriate to the impending trial of a witch, not to mention convenient: the trial was be held at Avaricum within walking distance. Once the eponymous capital of Bituriges founded by the indigenous Gauls, Avaricum was destroyed and its inhabitants slaughtered by Caesar's army not long before the birth of our Lord. To reach it and the inn nearby the *curé* advised following along rue Bourbonnoux, notable for being lined with half-timbered houses, and after a time asking a citizen for further directions.

Having discharged his priestly duty of courtesy to strangers, any of whom might be Jesus in disguise, he dropped his eyes and crossed himself, ashamed of having uttered the name of the Dark Prince. With nothing more to offer he hurried to the other side of the street and disappeared down a narrow alley, sandals slapping on the cobbles. The tribunal would be ecclesiastical under jurisdiction of the Church, managed out of the Archidiocèse de Bourges with offices in the famous Cathédrale Saint-Étienne de Bourges, which the priest had said we would pass along the way. As its name so states the Cathédrale is dedicated to Saint Stephen, Christianity's first martyr.

We found the inn on rue Parerie where the innkeeper, a grimy disheveled man with a shifty eye, provided more information about the city. The upper and lower sections of Bourges, he said, are separated by Roman ramparts, and the present population he estimated at about fifteen thousand citizens. The man was short, no more than a half-head taller than I, who am no taller than a midget and rotund as a barrel. He had the annoying mannerism of keeping his hands close to his chest and rubbing them together obsequiously, all the while bending forward. This had the effect of making himself appear even smaller, and apparently more harmless. I distrusted him immediately and vowed to watch my goods and expenditures even closer than usual. Innkeepers are notorious cheats, the urban equivalent of highway robbers.

I said my colleague would arrive at any moment and that we would not tolerate unclean food, filthy bedding, and French wine adulterated with green Spanish swill.

We expected lodging and fare fit for noblemen and wine of a decent and purely French vintage. For the duration of our stay my colleague and I would share a bed and require a table in the tavern reserved for our two daily meals and evening relaxation. Our sleeping quarters must be vermin-free, a near impossibility in modern France but nonetheless worth demanding.

My men, I said, were to be housed in a vacant stall in the stable with fresh hay and receive their two daily meals there. The thin fellow on the donkey, my personal servant, was in charge and gave orders to the two footmen. Breakfast for each, to be delivered to their quarters by a serving girl, must consist of a bowl of small beer, a small loaf of barley bread, a block of cheese, and hot tea. For the evening meal, soup with meat, cabbage or potatoes, a small loaf of barley bread, a block of cheese, hot tea, and two flagons of Spanish wine to share among them. I emphasized that the taller footman would connive to increase his measure of wine, offering to pay from his own pocket, but be assured his pockets are empty and my own sewn shut to this demand.

Finally, my animals required this summer's hay, not last year's cut, and water, of course. My colleague's horse would be stabled with my palfrey, and my men would see to their care, including the mucking of their stalls. No other expenses were to be added to my account, which would be checked carefully at departure. I emphasized that Monsieur Révigny and I were lawyers of the king's court and would guarantee his immediate bankruptcy, confiscation of his property, and expulsion of his family into the street if he tried to cheat us.

Révigny, as always, simply appeared soon after

nones riding what appears to be an ordinary looking horse, although actually a docile demon. It requires no care, but consumes whatever food and water are offered. Demons don't need to eat or drink, and they don't shit, so mucking after it would not be necessary. Jamet took the horse and stabled it beside my palfrey, which either failed to recognize its other-worldly status or didn't care. Everything would go smoothly. François and Alvin take everything in stride, so long as they aren't challenged or frightened and their own essential animal needs are fulfilled. Jamet, as mentioned before, became accustomed to demons during his period as a wandering beggar when he lived for a time in a haunted forest and found hobgoblins, at least, to be harmless and stupid.

Révigny and I went to the tavern and ordered wine. There was little purpose to a formal greeting; only a few days had passed since the werewolf trial ended. We simply raised our cups from across the table in a silent toast to the upcoming adventure. His lips formed a faint, fleshy rictus momentarily stuck against a bare skull, but the image was fleeting, quickly disappearing behind sulfurous smoke, then he settled into his chair causing a momentary disruption in the stasis of reality. The air inside his "cocoon" jiggled with any activity, setting in motion the smoke that always swirled and followed these movements after a slight delay. Everything contained inside bounced against the fluid boundaries of his outline. It was like airy jelly shaking. The disturbance soon subsided, the elements regaining composure. Everything, that is, except me. Watching this was always unnerving.

"How was your meeting with the Four Horsemen of the Apocalypse?" said Révigny. It was a question hardly needing an answer.

"You know, so why ask?"

"I know whatever I need to know." He smirked at me, eyes flashing amber. "You realize, of course, that they wouldn't have been visible had all participants not been dead."

"Really? But Jamet saw them too and dived for cover underneath the donkey. And François and Alvin galloped away on the mule."

Jamet is also dead. He died during the *mêlée* in the public square at Magny-Cours after the werewolf trial. He doesn't yet know. François and Alvin were responding to Jamet's behavior. Life still flows through those two. You've had glimpses of the other side, such as during your ride through the haunted forest on the way to Magny-Cours. Only someone destined for Hell could have seen the green eyes of those hobgoblins or even sensed their presence. You'll see more as time passes and you get closer to an audience with Satan. Understand that for the time being Satan has tapped you to oppose me in court during the upcoming trial of this witch at Bourges. That was the plan all along. Any further metamorphosis of your insubstantial state must wait. And Jamet, you recall, regularly conversed with hobgoblins in that haunted forest well before he was killed at Magny-Cours, strong evidence his ultimate destination had been preordained too."

I pondered this. It all seemed so strange. "The Four Horsemen were nothing like I'd have expected, although admittedly I never thought about them much in life. They appeared almost clownish, except Death. He was truly scary. Anyway, they weren't the muscular, fearsome warriors depicted in the illustrations and paintings. They actually looked bedraggled and harmless. And exhausted. Yes, that's the word. Exhausted."

"Wandering for centuries can induce that effect," Révigny said.

"They told me a story about the blacksmiths and potters of Abyssinia who turn themselves into hyenas at night and terrorize the population."

Révigny looked at me thoughtfully and changed the subject. "You realize, Barthélemy, that the burning of brimstone might have been the only plague preventive that actually worked? I can't recall ever encountering a case of *la peste noir* in Hell. Probably the heat or because the inmates are dead." At this he laughed himself into a violent coughing fit. After it subsided, he continued: "Even funnier, Guy de Chauliac, physician to Pope Clement VI and head of the medical school at Montpellier, advised the pope to burn sulfur in his chamber and sit between two fires kept lit night and day during the height of the plague years. My gracious, his environment seems oddly familiar. I wonder, was Doctor Chauliac preparing His Holiness for the heat and sulfurous fumes he might later meet in the netherworld? Ah, who can say? This we know for certain: brimstone smoke inhaled directly does have a downside, although eventually you come to love it." He stood and spread his arms. "How can anyone resist the sweet aroma of Hell's perfume?"

Révigny again took his chair. "These Four Horsemen of the Apocalypse, they were Normans?"

"Yes."

Révigny leaned back. "Normans, I've heard, practice a peculiar method of social bonding similar to hyenas. They howl and laugh through the night then gather the next morning to take a communal shit." With this he slapped the table and howled.

I ignored the outburst. "Were they even real?" The innkeeper's wife had just poured us each another cup of wine. This time I concentrated on its taste. The vintage was ordinary, but unadulterated.

"Interesting ontological question. 'Reality' is a state embodying. . .what? Doubly interesting when posed by one specter to another concerning a meeting with four other specters and observed by a fifth. That would be Jamet, of course. The best answer is, yes and no." He reached out and gave my shoulder an avuncular pat, a gesture without haptic sensation on my end and probably his too. Hardly surprising, I suppose, when one ghost touches another, although our touches seem real enough to the living, to which François could attest after the scourging I gave him yesterday, our first at the inn, for attempting to beg wine from one of the serving girls.

Notice of our arrival would soon reach the court. We had nothing to do but await word when the trial would start. A court messenger might appear at any time. Révigny scanned the room, twisting his head completely around without moving his torso, a feat not even an owl could mimic. "The wine is decent," he said, at that moment facing me. "You had our standard talk with the new innkeeper, right?"

"Don't you know?"

"Too mundane. I didn't bother listening."

"I gave him the standard instructions, and he seems suitably terrified. Soon we shall know if the food is edible. Jamet, François, and Alvin are comfortably ensconced in the stable. Jamet has been Heaven-sent."

Révigny twirled his empty cup absently on the table top and signaled for the innkeeper's wife to fill it. "Interesting case, Jamet's. I remember his story, of course, how he attacked your donkey in the haunted forest on the road to Magny-Cours, attempting to steal food from one of its packs. You ended up engaging him as your personal servant. Quite a happy ending! He proved stalwart during that *mêlée* in the town square following the werewolf trial, helping clear a safe path for us through the public market. Satan will surely reserve a place for him at your side if you care to bring him. He allows servants to stay with their masters and continue performing their duties provided their histories meet his low standards, and Jamet's past obviously does. A priest defrocked for having carnal relations with a married woman in his parish surely qualifies. Add random fornication with prostitutes, performing magic acts for monetary gain in public squares, attempted thievery from a member of the landed gentry. . . ." He gave his hollow laugh that reverberated from the floor upward like a misappropriated echo.

I thought about the Four Horsemen and how unlikely they seemed. Not just that, but the harrowing tale of *la peste noire*. I said, "No doubt the Black Death is a popular fireside topic in Hell."

Révigny sat back, hands clasped behind his head, and gazed up thoughtfully. "Indeed so. It was a time of

cheap death. People took up wallowing in sin and lassitude, forgetting what few morals they had. All levels of
French society became lax, although not moreso than
the rest of Europe. At least we French have a beautiful
language with which to express our perversities unlike,
say, the Germans and English. What ugly sounds they
make! Hardly the music of poetry and theater. More
like the love songs of rutting hogs and angry rooks.

"Don't forget, Barthélemy, that Satan knows all the
workings of Heaven, including who qualifies for entry.
He was once head angel and went by the name Lucifer
until expelled by God. You could say that Satan spent
his early eternity there." He started to laugh at this
little joke, but immediately collapsed into a spasm of
violent coughing. He bent over double, and I watched
his frail shoulders heave. The grin flashed just before
was the usual macabre rictus, at once sinister and sad.
I thought for a moment he might puke, then remembered that spirits can't digest and otherwise process
food and drink, making such a thing impossible. The
coughing subsided. Révigny stood, smoothed down his
tunic, and then began muttering, to himself it seemed.

He stopped this abruptly, sat, and resumed our conversation. "Just to get under the skin of devout Christians, Satan often shows sympathy to Catholicism's
pariahs, notably freemasons, Protestants, and Jews.
However, as you know his principal fixation is death,
particularly in the moment it occurs. By the time a soul
arrives in Hades he's long since lost interest. One dis-
embodied soul burning at a stake and shrieking in pain
is the same as the next. You could even say that Satan
considers his greatest *oeuvre* to be snatching souls as

they rise from their bodies at the instant of death, then pushing them gently toward Purgatory where most can anticipate their final destination, as he delicately puts it, 'home.' So yes, we talk about the Black Death often and see many examples of its rampages writhing in the fires around us. Satan often jokes that the Black Death's most lasting tragedy has been hastening the decline in good fashion sense. The better classes haven't dressed with the same élan in the years since and doubtless never will." He sighed and turned to look at me. "The days when Paris was the fashion center of the civilized world are long gone, never to return.

"You've asked before what Satan looks like. I'll repeat: anyone or anything he chooses. A pig or a priest, a bumblebee or a whale. He has the libido of a satyr, the compassion of an inquisitor, and he's happiest when observing humans at their most base, which explains his fondness of wars, famines, and plagues, personified by the lesser three horsemen in Saint John's vision of the Apocalypse. The fourth and most delightful, of course, is Death because he encompasses the other three. Many have seen the Devil in one of his countless guises. He has knocked on many doors, and some have wrestled with him. Martin Luther threw his inkwell at Satan but missed, leaving a tell-tale stain on a wall inside his house. Pilgrims ever since have visited the site regularly to pray. Of course, we would expect a Protestant to have poor aim.

"Let's isolate plagues, or epidemics as some call them, and investigate their effects in greater depth. In addition to widespread death these events cause peculiar expressions of morality just as strange, contagious, and frightening as the physical manifestations. Mankind reverts to his primitive origins and out pop those inborn qualities of the barbarian: cruelty, revenge, blood-thirstiness, tribalism, and, most startling, slavish loyalty and obedience before equally deranged leaders who seem to arise spontaneously, like toadstools. These traits are then manifested in sloganeering and persecution of minorities, defined as any member of the Other, and culminate in public rage, destruction of property, and murder.

"Not many centuries ago Europe experienced the Children's Crusades, dancing manias and similar episodes of mass chorea, the rise of the flagellates, and vicious persecution of the Jews. Today we continue to torment Jews, but also discharge these base impulses through demon phobias and the burning of witches. Ah, the wonders wrought by civilizing influences like the Church and its leaders! How could Satan not be thrilled? God works night and day restocking those creations in His image. So much clay to be molded, breathed into life, then ultimately scorched in the fires and reduced to ashes and grease. Contemplate how many thousands—no, millions—have been slaughtered over the centuries in the name of one religion or another. The true numbers, were we to ever determine them, would be breathtaking, no?"

Casual conversation finished, we turned to the trial ahead. The presiding judge would be Institoris, author of *Malleus maleficarum* (*Witch-Hammer*), the standard text for persecuting and prosecuting witches, and Europe's cruelest and most infamous inquisitor. It was the rare defendant who emerged from his court and escaped death at the fiery stake. The woman accused in the pending case—a girl, actually—was Mademoiselle Ambrosine Sécretain, born at Bourgon in northwestern France, the daughter of a vineyard worker now deceased. She had given her age as fifteen years. I knew nothing else about her except what was contained in the pretrial documents delivered to Révigny and me at the end of the werewolf trial at Magny-Cours. My instructions simply were to proceed directly to Bourges and defend this Mademoiselle Sécretain charged with witchcraft.

I would have to steer her defense carefully without trapping myself in heresy's mire, a much less serious problem considering I am already dead. Anyway, a lawyer who defends an accused witch must not deliver his arguments too vigorously and restrain himself from righteous statements in support of his client. Paradoxically, guilt must be assumed and any notion of presumptive innocence set aside. Mercy in these cases is defined as negotiating with the judge to allow the executioner to strangle his client, thus obviating the excruciating pain of live immolation. Yes, I must tread lightly and dampen any enthusiasm or pity I might feel rising inside me. As the *Malleus* states: *If the counselor defends his suspected client too warmly, it is right and reasonable that he should be considered as far more criminal than the sorcerer or the witch herself; that is to say, as the protector of witches and heretics he is more dangerous than the sorcerer. He should be looked upon with suspicion in the same degree as he makes a zealous defense.* These very words were penned by Institoris. Ignoring them would be foolhardy. On the other hand, why should I care what Institoris believed? What could he possibly do to me? Nothing. So, beware Monsieur Institoris, of a few perfectly aimed and well-worded insults hurled your way after the masterly style of Humbert de Révigny at whose knee I've learned so thoroughly.

The next day, Friday the 19th of October, Révigny and I met in the tavern at terce for breakfast, then took a stroll through the streets of Avaricum to locate the municipal building where the tribunal would be held and estimate the time necessary to reach it on foot. Considering the short distance there was no reason to saddle our horses.

It was a square, austere building of one storey constructed of gray fieldstones crudely assembled and patched over with a patina of colorful lichens. We identified ourselves to a guard, who led us inside. No trial was in progress, so the single large room of about seven meters square was empty except for its spare furnishings. A long table opposite the door had been pushed nearly against the wall leaving barely adequate space behind for chairs to seat the judge, prosecutor, and attorney for the defense. Our backs would be almost touching the cold stones. Two meters or so in front of the table was a rectangular dock of some two meters square, to its right a small table and chair for the clerk of the court. From the way the earthen floor was packed hard and rose to meet the walls at the edges it was apparent that spectators filled the place when trials were in session. On dry days the spectators' feet would stir up dust; on rainy days the floor would turn to mud. Within such close confines the atmosphere promised to be noisy and chaotic.

Trials, which are open to everyone, are often held

outside castle or city gates. Another common venue is the public square, a convenient place where people gather to socialize, express their grievances, shop at the stalls and kiosks, conduct business, and be entertained. The diocese apparently ruled against holding this event outdoors with winter just around the corner.

Révigny and I spent the weekend relaxing and reviewing the case and on Monday morning, October 22nd and a little prior to terce we entered the court to meet Institoris, now a celebrity feared and admired throughout Europe for the ferocity with which he pursues and burns witches. He proved to be a slightly built man with a pinched face, unsmiling mouth, and quick darting eyes. "Monsieur Barthélemy de Chassenée," he said. "I am familiar with your work. Are you acquainted with the Church's advocate Monsieur Humbert de Révigny?"

"I've known him most of my professional life," I said. "That is, I *had* known him prior to my, uh, why yes, I have known him quite a long time."

"Yes, I see." Institoris seemed put off by my sudden hesitation and switching of tenses. I glanced at Révigny in time to see the trace of a smirk vanish from his face. "And you, Monsieur Prosecutor, are you as well acquainted with the attorney for the defense as he claims to be with you?"

"Yes, Your Grace. We have crossed swords many times. Monsieur Chassenée is both a cherished friend and a formidable opponent."

"Very well, then. No further words in this regard are required, and I need only introduce you to the clerk of the court, the bailiff, and the bailiff's men." Which he did by restating our names and responsibilities while everyone stood, Révigny to his right, me to his left, the clerk against the adjacent wall closest to Révigny, and the dock directly in front of Institoris. The room had been filling with spectators since early morning and was nearly packed. Still more gawkers pressed in while we waited, rapidly shrinking the space and turning it claustrophobic. The atmosphere quickly became stuffy and oppressive from the combination of foul breath and body odors. People were standing and sitting everywhere, eating and drinking, laughing, arguing, gossiping, and spitting. Children and drunks urinated where they squatted or stood. The door and all four windows, one in each wall, had been blocked open to allow a change of air, however paltry. As the spectators settled down, denizens of the barnyards and alleys crept timidly through the door, hunger and hope overcoming their natural fear of mankind: pigs and stray dogs, a mangy cat accompanied by three adolescent kittens, a goat, and a rooster, all intent on scavenging scraps. They would be competing with several shabby beggars.

We members of the court sat waiting for the signal allowing the tribunal to open and soon heard it, the bells of Cathédrale Saint-Étienne de Bourges tolling the hour of terce. With fading of the final reverberations Institoris stood and raised his hand for silence. It was a near-royal gesture given by a man accustomed to deferential treatment. He said, "Tribunals such as this are a direct mandate from God directing the Church to carry out its duty to fend off works of the Dark Prince implemented through his uncountable minions. Witches must be pursued wherever they conduct their evil deeds, to the ends of the Earth, if necessary.

The words of Jean Bodin taken from his great treatise *De la démonomanie des sorciers,* known to scholars as the Code of Bodinus, is a standard against which we judge defendants accused of witchcraft. I quote: *The trial of this offense must not be conducted like other crimes. Whoever adheres to the ordinary course of justice perverts the spirit of the law, both Divine and human. He who is accused of sorcery should never be acquitted unless the malice of the prosecutor be clearer than the sun; for it is so difficult to bring full proof of this secret crime, that out of a million of witches not one would be convicted if the usual course were followed!"*

And so the line was drawn. The established rules of evidence would be ignored in the interest of expediency, specifically the rush to conviction and execution. My client would be boxed in from the start by Institoris' blatantly biased opening statement attributed to Bodin, fellow persecutor of witches. For practical purposes Mademoiselle Ambrosine was already tied to the stake; the flint had only to be struck, the kindling ignited. I could do little except prolong her trial and hope for a miracle. To date, Institoris had sent hundreds of putative witches to their deaths, and he was still a young man, his career just reaching stride. The task ahead appeared hopeless.

I had another obstacle to overcome on behalf of the client, something personal. It arose the first day of any such public proceeding. I refer to my horrid physical appearance, which puts me at immediate disadvantage, prejudicing the gallery and often the judge and contaminating their opinions of the person whose very life depends on my ability to convince them otherwise.

For the first several days I am subject to open ridicule and hostility by the spectators, recipient of cruel taunts and laughter and not infrequently the target of rotten vegetables when my words conflict with the ignorant beliefs and superstitions of the masses.

Not for a moment has anyone considered me attractive, desirable, or even threatening. Born an ugly baby, I died an ugly adult. Truly, a common garden toad has more appeal. In me, people encounter a face that although mostly hidden behind a beard is nonetheless marked horribly by scars from childhood smallpox. Then consider my oversized Gallic nose, also pockmarked and riven with broken blood vessels, the manifestations of many nights attempting to drink myself handsome and respected. Expressionless porcine eyes look out at the world inviting doubt and suspicion. As if these features were not detrimental enough, factor in a torso dominated by a massive paunch juxtaposed obscenely against the stature of a child. To my advantage are a burning suspicion and disdain of humanity, a sharp analytical mind, and an adequate education, the latter bestowed by parents fortunate to have been born into the merchant class. These traits and accomplishments had been sufficient to see me through a largely unsatisfying and unhappy life, although one of considerable financial success.

I had been musing pensively on my estate when a change in the inflection of Institoris' voice returned me abruptly to the immediate scene. He had begun to speak about something dear to him. "A witch requires no formal learning to practice her craft, being empowered entirely by Satan through his demons. The breadth of her knowledge is not limited by age. The witch to be tried here—and you shall see her soon in the dock—is young and innocent in outward appearance, not someone we might consider capable of pure evil, although I assure you her heart is hard and cold as a tombstone. Like others of her sort she honed her evil powers at nocturnal gatherings with other witches, the so-called sabbaths where demons and often Satan himself instruct them in the black arts. By this means witchcraft has gradually become feminized and distinguished from necromancy, a mostly male fraternity of participants.

"From an inquisition at Toulouse we have the first instance in which the Church acknowledges the reality of a witches' sabbath. The story is told by Anne Marie de George and her sister Catherine, both ladies advanced in years who in separate confessions admitted to worshipping Satan at such gatherings over some twenty years. Anne Marie's story is particularly interesting. She noted that one morning when she was washing clothes near Peche-David a man of monstrous size came toward her over the water trailing an odor of burning brimstone mingled with the stench of a great beast in rut. His skin was black, as if burned to charcoal by intense fire, his eyes red like smoldering coals. He was dressed in animal skins, and as he came nearer the iron cross she wore on a chain turned so hot she instinctively ripped it from her neck and threw it away. He asked if she would give herself to him, but whether the request was made by voice or thought she was unsure. His power was so strong that she readily agreed. After sex he blew into her mouth.

"A week later she was transported through the air

to a sabbath over which he presided, and where having assumed the form of a he-goat ravished her again. In the coming months and years at these gatherings he taught her secret incantations, the use of poisons, methods of surreptitiously defiling the Host during communion, and how to cast spells, all this to promote evil and sacrilege and denigrate the Savior. She and her fellow acolytes in the company of Satan and his demons boiled foul items together in a bubbling cauldron over a flame that Satan had cursed. The ingredients used to make their potions and unguents included toxic herbs, remnants of bodies buried in consecrated ground, pieces of rope from hanged criminals, the bones and fat of unbaptized babies they had just cooked and consumed. They learned how to murder persons they disliked through image magic, such as shaping wax figures of them, which they laid on a hot brazier or pierced with needles. A person so cursed soon wasted away and died.

"Her sister told similar stories. On Friday nights she fell into deep slumber in which state which she flew through the air to appointed sabbaths, some held nearby, others in the far Pyrenees, still others in countries she had never seen where the languages, customs, and costumes were strange. There they feasted on newborn babies or slightly older children stolen from their cribs. The liquids served were repugnant. The fare was without taste and failed to fill the belly. It was like eating air.

"Sectaries gather for a sabbath on the appointed night, arriving on foot or riding demonic animals that run or fly to the predetermined place guided by Satan's directives. Some are transported on brooms or sticks of other sorts; it's said that a few even arrive seated comfortably in flying chairs. Some authorities posit that brooms and sticks must be treated with a special unguent before they can become airborne; others believe this is unnecessary and that simply straddling the object is sufficient. Animals of several kinds can serve as mounts, although never the donkey, excluded because of its part in Christ's passion.

"Once gathered at the predetermined site they openly worship Satan who, if he chooses to appear, can assume protean shapes. They usually worship him in his human form, kissing his feet and his cold, disgusting countenance. In loud wails they renounce Jesus, trample crosses, and spit and urinate on consecrated wafers symbolizing the body of the Host. A black cat usually accompanies Satan as his familiar, and at his command it crouches, raises its hindquarters, and invites Satan's acolytes to kiss its anus.

"At Satan's urging they murder infants and small children brought along to sacrifice, feasting on their flesh and drinking their blood. If more children have been brought than needed to feed the group, those in excess are boiled in a large cauldron together with toads and serpents. The distillate is then used to make unguents with bewitching properties. When the feast is finished the participants extinguish all candles used to illuminate the rituals, guzzle alcoholic spirits in the dark, and dance to exhaustion. The gathering devolves eventually into an orgy during which all sexual prohibitions are discarded, and those present wallow in carnal lust like rutting beasts, or *more brutorum*, copulating repeatedly with others of the same and opposite sex, with Satan and his demons, and with their familiars. One witch put on trial expressed astonishment that such activities are sinful. She thought she had been attending enjoyable and harmless pagan festivals! Imagine her surprise when the inquisitorial judge condemned her to be burned.

"I'll pause a moment and pose a question many have pondered: if Satan can act alone in causing any misery he chooses, why is he so eager to encourage witches? I can only speculate and offer this theory. It's probably more fun planning and then making mischief in the company of fellow believers than alone. And what more delightful venue for a being who embodies ultimate evil than a drunken orgy? And maybe a little ego is involved too. Like God, Satan insists on being worshipped and enjoys those times when surrounded by acolytes. Keep in mind that our god is a jealous deity. He says so in *The Book of Exodus*, chapter twenty verse five, again in chapter thirty-four verse fourteen, and in several other places in the Old Testament. Perhaps adding to Satan's glee God is deeply offended when one of His creations turns an evil deed. He expects no less of Satan but hopes for better from mankind, the beings created in His image. What could be more embarrassing than watching witches defile His glory?

"On Easter Sunday these witches, masquerading as wholesome village girls and women, attend Mass and receive the Host from the priest. Instead of swallowing it they carry it home hidden under their tongues where they spit it into the latrines, expressing the ultimate contempt of He who gave His life to save ours."

The crowd groaned on hearing of this blasphemy.

Institoris waited to let the meaning be absorbed before saying, "Monsieur Révigny will now present a brief overview of how witch trials are conducted, a necessary prelude for benefit of the court and gallery." He nodded at Révigny and sat.

Révigny rose and straightened his robe. "What I intend to present," he said, "is a historical synopsis for determining the guilt or innocence of those accused formally of witchcraft; that is, persons tried before a court of law. From earliest times demon worship was considered a form of heresy by the Church, and groups of witches were persecuted throughout the 13th and 14th centuries. Everyone knows how the Church treats heretics in this context. Someone denying belief in the reality of witches and demons is declared superstitious and burned at the stake. Admittedly, not everyone takes the existence of these beings seriously.

"Why does mankind place hope in supernatural powers and bow so readily to even the basest superstitions? Because the forces that control our lives are beyond human understanding. In a vain effort to circumvent pain and disease, convince someone to love us, avoid early death, enhance our crops, or dream of finding treasure in a random clod overturned by the plow many petition God and His angels to answer these needs. We pray for miracles. Not surprisingly, some put trust in conjurers, magicians, sorcerers, demons, even Satan. Is this really so strange when evil persists despite the Church's assurance that our Christian god protects and cares about everyone? Ah, witchcraft is no different from believing in God. Both have been erected in the vain effort to explain the unexplainable; or I should say unexplainable in our present state of intellectual development. Maybe the future will rid the world of superstition and full ratiocination will assume its place."

Institoris looked up. "Careful, Monsieur Prosecutor. You are dangerously close to stepping on heretical ground yourself."

Révigny bowed to the inquisitor and said, "My apologies, Your Grace," then turned back to face the spectators. "Starting in the 15th century and coinciding with the increasing number of witch trials, elements of ecclesiastical and secular proceedings were beginning to merge when animals were involved in what was perceived to be supernatural behavior. Instead of being anathematized, swarms of insects and schools of fish were increasingly sentenced to execution. A classic incidence of theriomorphism is the trial at Bâle in 1474 when magistrates sentenced a rooster to be burned at the stake. Presumably, a very short one," Révigny added after a pause, drawing a laugh from the audience. "And I quote: 'for the heinous and unnatural crime of laying an egg.' A large crowd watched solemnly as rooster and egg were torched. It was widely believed that the *oeuf cocatri* is an ingredient of witchly unguents. If such an egg is hatched by a snake the offspring might resemble a basilisk. If hatched by a toad, who could say? A basilisk, whatever its origin, reportedly ambushes humans, killing them with its dartlike vision.

"Legally, charges of *maleficium* have been associated with diabolical heresy and directed mainly toward cults that meet in secret to feast, dance, and worship demons, and often Satan himself, as His Grace mentioned. The participants become drunk and engage in orgies with their fellow cultists and with demons. In addition, they kidnap, murder, and devour babies and small children, preferably unbaptized, although not rejecting those who have been baptized. They also desecrate the cross by treading on it and defile consecrated wafers by spitting and urinating on them, acts not just sacrilegious but in terribly poor taste, not to mention imparting a poor taste to any devout Christians who might eat them." Révigny paused to grin at the audience, which rewarded his irreverence with laughter and heckling.

"Careful, monsieur," Institoris said. "Your presentation is becoming distasteful, at least to me."

Révigny again turned and bowed. "No pun intended, Your Grace, I'm sure." This went over the audience's head, although I couldn't resist chuckling and drawing Institoris' stony glare. After a moment Révigny continued: "In the 12th and 13th centuries the method of prosecution was accusatorial. Put simply, the aggrieved party was responsible for proving the accused's guilt. If the defendant was declared innocent the accuser was subjected to whatever punishment the person on trial would have received if declared guilty. This risk greatly limited frivolous accusations.

"Feudal lords, especially in countries to the east such as Hungary and Transylvania, were empowered to hold witch trials on their own and pass sentence, one of which could be trial by water. This occurred more often when witches were prosecuted in groups instead of individually. Trials and punishments were often *fait en entier*, leaving the accused no practical chance of exoneration, the outcome having been, in effect, predetermined and the trial merely for show.

"Witnesses commonly claim to have seen persons accused of witchcraft taking the form of birds, cats, or other creatures, and their testimonies are often believed by civil and ecclesiastical judges even in this more enlightened century. Consider the case of Anna Lázár, charged by officials with witchcraft in the Romanian town of Mikeháza. She was seen by different witnesses repeatedly entering her house as a hound, changing into a woman while indoors, and later emerging as a hound. Such a transformation is impossible to misinterpret and just as hard to refute. She was ordered to stand trial by water, to be acquitted if she sank, burned alive if she floated. This exercise contains a certain inherent logic, considering that a floating witch is less likely to drown than one who sinks. In what form was Madame Lázár tried, a dog or a woman? The record doesn't say." This brought a loud collective guffaw from the audience.

"Monsieur, I'll not warn you again," said Institoris. "As prosecutor it isn't your place to question the methods used to ascertain the innocence or guilt of those practitioners of witchcraft."

Again, Révigny turned and bowed. "I presume His Grace refers to those *accused* of practicing witchcraft but not yet convicted." He then continued with seeming nonchalance. "However, most cases of witchcraft are difficult to demonstrate if the legal proceeding is fair, and the accused might be made to undergo a trial in which God and not man judges and decides the outcome. From the 12th century to the present both ecclesiastical and secular courts have gradually abandoned the accusatorial method and adopted the inquisitorial system, like the trial about to commence. Within such a framework the burden of innocence or guilt becomes the responsibility of the court instead of the accuser. In addition, the court can initiate inquisitorial investigations and trials independently of an accusation, or even in its absence. Because eyewitnesses to crimes involving *maleficium* are rare the objective has become eliciting the accused's confession, without which a guilty verdict can't be pronounced. Torture is considered the truth-seeking instrument *nonpareil* based on the belief that nothing except pure truth can emerge with words screamed out in excruciating pain. The uttering of a lie or half-truth, in other words, is not possible under such conditions, or so torture's tortuous reasoning goes. The technique and logic are borrowed from Roman law modified and justified in trying heretics on the principle that heresy is *crimen laesae majestatis divinae*, in the vernacular, 'treason against God.'"

Révigny turned to Institoris and bowed politely. "I remind His Grace that our own Saint Thomas Aquinas brought witchcraft into mainstream Christian dogma. He and his intellectual colleagues gave it a scholastic foundation justifying its reality, and with that came a formal means of identifying and prosecuting witches manifested in the Inquisition. People could subsequently be burned alive in the name of God.

"Witches became Satan's agents, their magical powers exceeding those of ordinary humans. Nicholas Eymeric became inquisitor of Aragon in the year of grace 1356. Twenty years later Eymeric published his procedural text *Directorium inquisitorum*, or *Directory of Investigation* in the vernacular, correlating witchcraft and heresy. The Church vigorously opposes any form of superstition. Christians who consort with demons or worship or show them the honor of *dulia* is guilty of apostasy. Such persons, if having been baptized, are heretics by default.

"The final link securing this ineluctable chain was supplied in the year of grace 1486 with publication of the most advanced and sophisticated work yet produced on witches and their prosecution. This is *Malleus maleficarum*, *Witch-Hammer* in the vernacular, written by Heinrich Godfrey Krämer, also known as Institoris, which is Latin for Krämer. The first chapter opens with the words, *Whether the belief that there are such beings as witches is so essential a part of the Catholic faith that obstinately to maintain the opposite opinion manifestly savors of heresy.* Therefore, not only is anyone practicing witchcraft a heretic, so is anyone who doesn't believe that witches and witchcraft exist.

"With the texts of Eymeric, Institoris, and those authored by others, Church authorities now had at hand an ecclesiastical typology to consult, a complete taxonomy of witches and witchcraft. Their secrets had to be exposed, their blasphemies, evil rites empowering *maleficia*, and objectives made known. Witches are a threat not just to the communities where they live, but to Christendom worldwide. No longer would evil hold good Christians in terror. Empowered with restrictive laws and punishments we could catalog their crimes and legislate appropriate punishments; Satan's armies stood no chance against rational man backed by God Himself. We could identify witches, hold them responsible, and prosecute them for the innumerable calamities that arise in everyday life: hailstorms, floods, crop failure, the hurling of curses real and imagined, human and livestock diseases, male sexual impotence, and female frigidity. Demon infestations accounted for madness, murder, and birth deformities. Demons expanded our fears of darkness and whatever torment the mind could imagine. Evil had crept closer, but now the inquisitors could keep it safely at bay.

"We know from Saint John's *Book of Revelation* how Satan lost that war in Heaven with the Archangel Michael and his forces, who in effect clipped his wings and sent him spiraling down to Earth. But Satan had many followers of his own who accompanied him, and we know two things about them: their myriad numbers and their capacity to have sex with humans. What could the Church do? Exorcise them, of course.

"Pope Innocent VIII issued a papal bull against witchcraft in the year of grace 1484 that extended absolute power to Heinrich Krämer, his appointee as master inquisitor and known to all as Institoris, the great man who authored *Malleus maleficarum* and presently presides over this proceeding. Members of the gallery, you are privileged to be in his presence." Révigny turned toward Institoris and languidly held out his hand, which the latter acknowledged with a nod and hint of a smile. "The bull made decisions of such papal appointees final and irrefutable. Appeals are not permitted, not to other courts, not even to the pope himself, God's supreme representative on Earth. In effect, Institoris and his colleagues were granted the power to implement capital *supplicium* under any conditions as they see fit. To repeat, *their decisions are without recourse and irreversible.*

"The *Malleus* of Institoris consolidated rules for trying witches into a single volume. Among the more salient of these establishes that a trial can commence without previous accusation, as I've discussed. In addition, testimony of known reprobates, excommunicants, and previously convicted criminals is allowed." Révigny paused and looked out over the audience. Then he said forcefully: "*In other words, the oaths of persons that under other circumstances would not be credible are accepted in cases against someone accused of witchcraft.* Furthermore, if a witch's lawyer seems overly eager in defending his client he too is susceptible to charges of witchcraft. As to procedure the accused is sometimes put to the rack *before* the trial starts as inducement to tell the 'truth.' At some locations torture is permitted if a citizen is even suspected of witchy behavior, according to the Code of Bodinus and another devised by Henry Boguet, self-proclaimed Grand Judge of Witches for the Territory of St. Claude. Rewards for every witch convicted has resulted in a new vocation, that of professional witch hunter.

"Inquisitions jettisoned accusatorial trials in which accusers faced penalties for failing to substantiate their charges. This was a great aid to prosecutors because trials for witchcraft made proving charges difficult, considering a bewitching might be delayed or initiated from some distance away making even establishing the scene of the crime impossible. Remember that case at Strasbourg? A man accused a woman of weather magic, and when unable to prove his charge was sentenced to be drowned. In those days not only did the accused face considerable risk, so did the accuser. Then inquisitorial procedures went into effect and judges both civil and ecclesiastical who didn't know a witch's broom from a tree branch could bring charges directly based on hearsay alone. And what an added blessing when witchcraft was merged with idolatry and apostasy, thus becoming a subcategory of heresy!

"Then that bitter enemy of witchcraft the Dominican professor of theology Johann Nider appeared on the scene. Among other gristly tales he described a coven of witches in Switzerland that had repudiated Catholicism and devoured at least thirteen babies. When authorities attempted to capture one of its number their hands trembled so violently they became unable to grasp her and were further repelled by a terrible odor. Nonetheless, a relentless judge succeeded in rounding up and burning most of the women. The event proved a wonderful example of God's power to fight evil in its many guises."

Institoris was clearly displeased with Révigny's presentation. It showed in how he looked down at the table while twirling his quill, his scowl twisted at the ends into a sort of grimace. It was the face of a bully plotting revenge. For what? The sarcasm? Or had the praise on his behalf been too faint? Institoris no doubt was expecting syrupy adulation, maybe a lengthy history of his professional accomplishments and their influence on mankind's timeless war against Satan. He probably had expected a panegyric outpouring of awe and received instead the bare-bones truth about the cruel deficiencies of his *Malleus* and the tracts of later writers who followed its example. Révigny had exposed his crowning achievement in words tainted with sarcasm and disgust, a reminder of how the result of prostituting the law to specific ends can be laid directly at the perpetrator's own feet. Maybe more apt, whirl around and with the swiftness of a serpent bite the perpetrator's ankle.

What Institoris could not have known, of course, is that Révigny as Satan's advocate would prefer to see more witches in the world, not fewer, and intensely disliked having them set alight and vaporized. Although he had been retained in this case to prosecute a particular witch, in truth it was our combined mission to save this young woman. "I've heard enough, Monsieur Révigny," said Institoris through clenched teeth. "Your time is up. Please be seated."

Clearly shaken, His Grace turned to his left and looked at me, now wary and uncertain how I might respond. If a prosecutor presumably in league with the Church had flipped so blatantly, how was the attorney for the defense likely to act? After seeming to study me a moment, he said, "You may now introduce what's on your mind as the client's representative, Monsieur Chassenée."

I rose to a chorus of hoots and catcalls directed mostly at my appearance and stood silently until the din attenuated. "Modern French courts still rely on 'theory of proof,' which refers to use of legal precedents by applying the logic that if opinions and judgments were the same in previous trials they should be the same now. The result is a framework within which former evidence and rulings constitute a standard, or precedent, relieving the judge of evaluating a case before him as 'novel' and thus lifting from him the burden of not weighing the evidence and circumstances in an unbiased way. Is this fair to both sides? Only if the precedents have proven fair and the present judge upholds that standard, rare circumstances for witch trials. Judges often rely on interrogatories, which are established leading questions that encourage or trick the defendant into self-incrimination. A competent defense lawyer must anticipate and recognize these unethical ploys and destroy them instantaneously before they can take root like poisonous weeds.

"To assure a 'fair' trial for a witch necessitates confession of guilt, ordinarily extracted by subjecting the accused to the rack or some other form of torture. So, of course, does one that's unfair. Is this lack of disparity a good thing? Hardly. Torture serves to induce pain that can be relieved only by removing its source. No sensible person actually believes that torture isolates and elicits 'truth.' None but idiots harbor such thoughts. A confession wrung from a tortured defendant simply reinforces the prejudices of judge and Church, parties in league and predisposed to convicting and then murdering the accused. Yes, *murdering* is the right term! Under what twisted system of logic can pain and truth be conflated? Was Christ's passion not holy? Did he not die for *us*? And was mankind not made in the image of God? The answers to these questions embody essential Christian truths, so how, please explain, do they encompass inflicting torture and pain on another human being? Consequently, how is torture justified by either God's laws or mankind's?"

Murmuring from the crowd now threatened to disrupt the proceeding, and Institoris rapped his mallet on the sounding block several times. He looked at me, eyes hardened by anger. "Watch how you speak, monsieur. It's right to defend your client, within limits. However, questioning inquisitorial trial methods is out of order, not to mention disrespectful to the Church and court."

I stared back and bowed without smiling. "Evidence of guilt might be proximate or remote," I said, brushing aside his remonstrance. "The former can be based on testimony of one or more witnesses, authenticated documents, extrajudicial confession, and other less weighty presumptions, such as the reliability of both witnesses and accused. The background and truthfulness of accusers and witnesses no longer matter, as Monsieur Révigny has just remarked, making their oaths worthless in the eyes of God, as they should be as well in the eyes of the Church and any inquisitional court. *As they should be among the most ignorant of us!*" I pounded my fist on the table. "Witnesses these days may be noblemen or paupers, good citizens or criminals, God-fearing or atheists. Anyone qualifies, leading me to ask, why should not self-declared witches be eligible to testify on behalf of a purported witch on trial for witchcraft? What could be more witchy? And how could it be illegal?"

Institoris jumped to his feet. "Monsieur, that will do! Weigh your words carefully or I shall find you in contempt and jail you with your client. You are very close to heresy."

I bowed again. "Not so close as you think, Your Grace. But back to proximate and remote evidence. The latter is weaker and might involve the accused's physical appearance or behavior in the dock. Some people just look or act guilty. But as even the most stupid among us knows, appearances and actions can deceive. We have a cultural image of witches as crones riding broomsticks through the night sky silhouetted against the moon, isn't that so?" I pointed to the gallery and waited for a response.

"Yes!" someone shouted.

"Then drag any harmless crone—any grandmother—into the dock," I said. "Go ahead. It's presently empty and awaiting a victim. Dress her in black, place a pointed hat on her head and a broomstick in her hand, and how would you in the gallery respond?"

"Burn the witch! Torch her to ashes!" they shouted.

"But," I said, holding up my hand for quiet, "the caveat is the confession. To be convicted she must confess to the crimes of which she's accused. How can the court be certain a confession is forthcoming? By putting her to the rack, of course! And if actually innocent is her so-called 'confession' then an admission of truth or merely acknowledgment of unbearable pain?

"The most common method of executing demons and witches is by burning, but at trial many methods other than the rack have been deployed to confirm guilt. The Code of Hammurabi from Mesopotamia dates to the 3rd century before birth of our Lord and is among the earliest. In ancient Babylonian trials by water an accused person who drowned was guilty, which conveniently conflated trial, judgment, and conviction in a single event. Trial by water—all ordeals, in fact—were banned in the year of grace 1215 at the Fourth Lateran Council, but many have persisted into modern times. The contemporary term of this one is 'the swimming of witches,' and although the accused are denied an actual opportunity to swim the procedure is occasionally effective at preventing or ending droughts and useful in this regard." The audience laughed. I glanced at Institoris and saw his face sour. He kept silent but continued twirling his quill. I went on as if unaware of his agitation. "Quite often the swimming of witches has been employed when guilt is questionable, or at least obscured, as in cases of adultery and casting of spells. The method obviously is meant as punishment, a drowning victim having no chance of redemption."

Institoris stopped fidgeting and started to speak. "Monsieur. . . ." But I spoke over him before he could continue and resumed my monologue. His Grace did nothing to stop me.

"In modern times the order of innocence and guilt has been reversed: the innocent sink and the guilty float. Why? Obviously, a weightless body is being buoyed by demons. Furthermore, because witches reject baptism's sacred waters it stands to reason that water in turn will reject them, causing them to bob on the surface instead of being clutched in a wet embrace and pulled under.

"I shall describe the 'swimming of a witch' for those who have never witnessed it. The accused's right thumb is tied to her left big toe, her left thumb to her right big toe. A rope is looped around her waist, the ends held by two men, one standing on either side. The accused is then tossed into a pond or river. If she floats this signifies that the 'sacred water of baptism' has rejected her because of her crimes. If she sinks it's a sign of God's aqueous medium having accepted her, thus demonstrating innocence.

"The entire experience retains a vague link to baptism when a child might sink and drown. In this sense the rite of baptism is a trial. The baptismal font can be deep, four meters or more. Fumbling the child at the instant of its immersion places it at genuine risk. Most babies are sinkers, thus proving beyond doubt their acceptance to God's bosom.

"Then there's trial by poison. An innocent person vomits, a guilty one dies. In both situations the legal charges typically center on the casting of malign spells or lechery, witchcraft at its most foul. Trials by poison of Hebrew women accused of adultery are recorded in the Old Testament *Book of Numbers*, chapter five verses eleven to thirty-one. A wife so accused is cursed by the priest in the tabernacle and made to drink 'bitter water': *And when he hath made her to drink the water, then it shall come to pass, that, if she be defiled, and have done trespass against her husband, that the water that causeth the curse shall enter into her, and become bitter, and her belly shall swell, and her thigh shall rot; and the woman shall be a curse among her people.* The 'thigh' is a misplaced reference to the womb. Isn't everything foul and evil somehow tied to sex and reproduction?

"Another test is what we might call 'trial by imp.' An 'imp' is any sort of tiny demon. The accused is made to sit quietly in a jail cell in an uncomfortable posture without food or drink for a day and a night. Guards are posted to see if Satan or one of his imps pays a visit in the form of a flying insect. If the insect comes into the cell and escapes before the guards can kill it, then it must have been an imp. The accused is pronounced guilty and executed.

"In still a different test a suspect might be asked to recite the Lord's Prayer and if faltering or making a mistake is at once declared guilty and executed. Other methods of determining the guilt or innocence of witches exist, but these are among the most common.

"Misogyny has been ingrained in the clergy from the beginning of Christianity based on Jesus having been a bachelor and presumably celibate, and Mary, his mother, a putative virgin. These assumptions make for awkward explanations of how Jesus came to acquire at least two brothers and an unknown number of sisters, their existence having been mentioned in *The Book of Mark*, chapter six verse three, and *The Book of Matthew*, chapter thirteen verses fifty-five and fifty-six. Maybe in Mary's case virgin birth was a one-time event.

"Paul advised avoiding women altogether, but if the urge to touch one became irresistible then marriage was the only tolerable amelioration for what was certainly a sinful and unpleasant situation. After all, marriage was better than burning in Hell for sinful thoughts and deeds. And if a man's wife should die it was a chance to regain composure and never marry again but stay celibate like our Lord and Savior. The ideal situation was for both women and men to remain virgin throughout their lives. The body is ugly, putrid, a portal for entry by demons that corrupt the soul.

"The conflation of *maleficium* and women became formalized with such publications as Johann Nider's *Formicarius*, or *The Anthill* in the vernacular, which appeared in the year of grace 1438. It fueled the burgeoning sport of witch-hunting. In another publication,

Praeceptorium divinae legis, or *Commentary on the Commandments* in laymen's language, Nider presented three canonical reasons for women's attraction to superstition. First, women are more credulous than men, a trait easily exploited by demons. Second, they are more impressionable and thus easily influenced. Third, they possess 'slippery tongues,' making them likely to spread the evil learned from others of their sex. Women are weaker than men intellectually, emotionally, and physically, encouraging their natural propensity for gullibility.

"This notion of women's inferiority is inconsistent on examination, considering that both sexes, educated or not, members of the clergy or the laity, believe equally in the reality of demons. Some of the Church's greatest minds confirm and reinforce this. Augustine of Hippo wrote that humans are incapable of producing supernatural or preternatural effects and must rely on intermediaries, and these, he concluded, could only be of demonic origin. By definition, anyone believing otherwise is bewitched.

"Nider's writings greatly influenced those who came later, especially the Dominican inquisitor Heinrich Godfrey Krämer, our own distinguished judge." I turned and extended an open hand toward him. Institoris set down his quill and nodded at the audience, which clapped and shouted appreciation of his acknowledgment. I waited for the noise to abate, then said, "His Grace's treatise *Malleus maleficarum* has been mentioned. Its contents offer detailed guidelines for inquisitors, including instructions for identifying, hunting, and capturing witches, and bringing them to justice. It represents the supreme example of clerical misogyny, and the Church must feel very proud. Needless to say, the *Malleus* has been enormously successful, assuring its author everlasting. . . *infamy*."

This last dig was too much. Institoris was clearly expecting a compliment, not a degrading remark. His response was cold and even. "Monsieur, I am sentencing you to spend the remainder of today and all of tonight with your client in her cell. There you might discover her true nature and emerge appreciating what she really is and having gained more respect for the court and for me." He shouted over the crowd to the back of the room. *"Bailiff, arrest this man! Court is adjourned!"* His mallet struck the sounding block with a loud crack.

I looked at Révigny. He was smiling broadly, eyes flashing brilliant red.

Chapitre cinq

Révigny and I had given lengthy opening statements, which made for a long day. The tolling bells of the Cathédrale now signaled vespers. Mademoiselle and I were sitting side by side on the wooden sleeping pallet in her cell. We had been together since just after nones when Institoris summarily adjourned court and ordered me trundled off to jail and into her cell. We were alone except for a bored jailer who sat picking his nose and watching us with sleepy eyes from his stool against the opposite wall. The bars retaining us were rusty with age and neglect, and the cell was a busy intersection of arachnid and insect life, disrupted occasionally by curious mice and rats pausing in their travels to study us. The atmosphere was cold and damp. Through the high window I saw the afternoon slipping through day's end toward darkness. Abruptly, the guard groaned and got stiffly to his feet, struck his flint and steel, and lit two lamps attached to sconces on opposite walls. The act was laborious and accompanied by considerable muttering. He was not a young man and seemed dull of wit.

My client, in contrast, was possessed of quick intelligence and disarming presence for a mere teenager. She had a lithe build, blonde hair that hung past her shoulders, and enormous blue eyes like deep pools. She was exceptionally pretty and had about her a fetching demeanor manifested in part by the clarity and precise articulation of her speech and how she looked her interlocutor in the eye while conversing, both characters unusual in one so young. They were expressions of self-confidence and a strong personality. Although barefoot and wearing only a thin tunic she seemed comfortable in our dank, chilly surroundings. Remarkably, she possessed all her teeth. When she smiled or laughed, which was often, they flashed brilliant white. I had been in her company only a short time and was already enamored. In truth, I found her bewitchingly unwitchy. The thought of such a worthy being expiring at a flaming stake was disheartening.

We had started discussing her situation, but stopped to watch the jailer light his lamps and listen to him bemoan his aching joints. When at last he sat down I turned to her and said, "Mademoiselle, we must now put aside idle talk and seriously discuss the trial and how I'm to defend you."

At that moment the door to the jail opened and an old woman shuffled in carrying a tray and a flagon of wine. "It's for them," she said, nodding in our direction. "His Lordship the prosecutor sends it." The jailer got painfully off his stool and unlocked our cell. The old woman set the tray and flagon on the pallet, bowed to me, and shuffled out.

"Are you hungry, mademoiselle?" I said.

"No. I don't need food."

"This comes from my colleague, Humbert de Révigny, and it's likely to be tasty, certainly superior to jail fare. How about some wine?" There were two cups on the tray. "It's an entire flagon, no doubt of decent French vintage."

"No, but go ahead."

"I don't want it either. Jailer," I said, "come and take away this tray. You may have both the food and the wine."

The man limped over. "Really, Your Lordship? That's very generous."

"Yes, really. Enjoy it."

Mademoiselle Ambrosine looked at me in silence, then said, "You may call me Ambrosine. After all, you're old enough to be my father. I would consider marrying you if you weren't so fat and ugly. Oh, and short, I nearly forgot. But I'd make certain we never had children. Be suspicious of every liquid you sip. It's common knowledge that a man can be made impotent if forced to drink a concoction of forty ants boiled in daffodil juice." She laughed, and the tone was again unexpected. Instead of an edgy, discordant cackle the sound was clear and pure as a perfectly cast bell.

These insults were only slightly perturbing. I was accustomed to harsh words from clients, usually uttered out of fear. It was best to change the subject with a quick diversion and then return to matters of the trial. "The name 'Ambrosine' means 'immortal.' Did you know that?"

"Yes. Fitting, don't you think? I was named after my grandaunt, who is still alive. . . somewhere. I think so, anyway."

"By 'somewhere' what do you mean?"

She shrugged and hugged her knees. "Everyone is terrified of Auntie Ambrosine because she's a witch, or was until they burned her. Probably still is. Last time I saw Auntie she was a crone, which made her look even scarier, all wrinkled and bent. Who wouldn't be after flitting here and there for centuries slinging curses around? Those unwise enough to piss off Auntie might find themselves croaking at the waxing moon from a lily pad or hopping through the evening dew covered with hideous warts. And they would be the lucky ones. The whole village avoids her, or did, except me. I was her apprentice. Where's Auntie now? I sense you about to ask. Who knows? The inquisitors believe they torched her, but she's certain to turn up meaner than ever."

"You speak as if your auntie is alive."

"Well, considering there was nothing left when the fire burned out—not a scrap of bone or even a tooth, no bit of clothing—what do *you* think? Plus, she went up in a puff of flame and smoke without a shriek. It was over in less than a minute. Human bodies don't burn that quickly. Everyone walked away puzzled."

"Mademoiselle—pardon me, Ambrosine, you must focus on the issues. We can't waste time in frivolous conversation. The accusations against you could not be more serious. I must be honest. In the absence of a miracle you will certainly receive a death sentence, likely a public burning. If that happens I'm willing to pay the executioner from my own pocket to strangle you first, at least sparing you the excruciating agony of the flames. I hope, of course, that Institoris shows a change of heart and pronounces a life sentence of incarceration on bread and water, but he's already sig-naled a strong dislike of me, which my sarcasm and disrespect have done nothing to dull."

She shifted on the pallet and looked at me. "You still don't understand. It makes no difference what the judge thinks, and neither does the sentence he pronounces. These matters are irrelevant because I won't be here." She stretched like a cat and yawned.

"How can you say you won't be here!" I stood and started pacing the floor, back and forth in front of her. She watched me in evident boredom. "You will obviously be here in this cell, locked up with the same vermin." I looked at her and gestured over my shoulder at the bars behind me. "And the jailer will be where he is now, sitting on the same stool a few meters away."

She said, "Notice the cockroaches and crickets? The mice and rats? And don't ignore the spiders. Some glow greenly. Can you see?" I nodded because some of them indeed had a greenish cast. "Those are demons. Think how easily I could bewitch the jailor into thinking I'd become one of them and slip away. And you," she said, "don't fool me in the least. You're a ghost. Within the hour our jailer will have drunk himself into a stupor and fallen asleep. We could simply disappear." Her voice trailed off, and she looked away. When she turned to face me again it was with a strange smile. "Except we shouldn't because matters are about to get interesting."

After a pensive moment she said, "According to the Master—excuse me, the prosecutor—witches walk among us. He's right, of course, but he failed to mention that so do the dead." She turned to me. "You know you're a dead man, but do you realize the prosecutor has come directly from Hell?"

"Yes," I said. "I understand my lifeless status, and I knew Révigny in life. I fail to grasp the relevance.

Someone surely placed us here. Satan? Why did you refer to Révigny as Master just now, and how do you claim to know what he said?"

"Never mind. A slip of the tongue." She stretched out her legs and looked at her feet, cocking her head this way and that and wiggling her toes. "It's all a play, a drama to amuse Satan. In fact, he's here somewhere watching the proceeding, probably from the gallery in the guise of a nobleman. As Monsieur Révigny no doubt told you that's Satan's *modus operandi*. Unless, of course, he's an actual participant. Nothing Satan appreciates more than a good play, and he considers himself quite the actor." She gave me a smile I can only call devilish. "If the truth were known, Satan isn't the everyman he claims to be. He loathes peasants and ranks them just underneath the clergy in his hierarchy of vileness."

I leaned my back against the wall. "Révigny has confessed this much to me. Naturally, I don't perceive him as a living being, but rather a demon or ghost wrapped in a cloud of burning brimstone smoke inside a marvelous, flexible cocoon. I'm curious about why I saw him like this when I was alive but nobody else did. And in death too, of course."

She said, "One of Satan's little tricks. I see Master the way you do, as a dead man stuffed clothes and all inside a gossamer skin, but there's more as you'll find out one day. Rumor says he pissed off a bishop, passed up last rites, and skipped along to Purgatory and beyond. God bless him, so to speak, for saying his mind regardless of consequences. And he acted that way *before* he was dead, or so his story goes. He claims he's made Hell's inner circle and gets furloughs up here to perform on stage when Satan gets bored. Ha! If only."

"Are you alive?" I said it suddenly, hoping to catch her unaware and gain a spontaneous answer, but she adeptly evaded the question.

"Figure it out yourself."

"And Institoris believes this is all happening on the level?"

"He's in the dark with the rest. He'd be shocked to watch this comedy through our eyes. Oh, and by the way, know that Master isn't fooled by any of it. He sees through this façade to the witch I truly am, which you still can't." She looked away and shrugged.

"Except it isn't so amusing," I said. "I'm concerned Institoris will sentence you to be burned alive. I've participated in lots of trials and usually know when a judge has already decided a case."

"So what? Then I won't show up for the final event. The outcome doesn't matter. Whether you or Master 'wins' is irrelevant, same as the sentence. Burn or walk, it hardly matters. Think of me as a chicken. If I'm sentenced to burn a brief ruckus will be heard from the chicken yard when the slavering hordes discover their object of torture and spectacle has flown the coop, and Institoris will tiptoe away with egg on his face, to continue the barnyard metaphors." She smiled at me with those empty blue eyes, jumped to her feet, and smoothed down her tunic. "So, enjoy the show, Monsieur Chassenée, and quit worrying."

CHAPITRE SIX

THE NEXT MORNING, THE second day of court, Ambrosine and I were let out of the cell and escorted under guard across the street to the municipal building where an excited crowd had gathered. Although a ghost, I seem substantial to the living and was duly treated as such by the bailiff's men, who pushed rudely through the rabble of gawkers, striking out with truncheons at those failing to step aside quickly. There were curses and shouts of pained surprise, but a path was cleared and we were whisked through the door. This was the first opportunity for the public to see Ambrosine, and everyone was astonished by her youth and beauty, many audibly gasping. She must have seemed dreamlike, a barefoot fairy princess disguised in a shabby tunic, but definitely no one's idea of a witch. Those already inside parted voluntarily, turning toward us mute and wide-eyed as she was led to the dock.

Révigny was sitting alone at the main table, Institoris having been temporarily delayed. He said to me in a low voice, "You look disheveled, monsieur. Did you miss your morning ablutions? And you smell vaguely caprine, like someone who has cavorted recently with goats."

"Shut up," I said, just as Institoris pushed in behind me and pulled out his chair.

After the tolling of the bells died away and the clerk declared court in session, Révigny asked and was granted permission to rebut my statements of the previous day. He rose from his seat and scanned the room waiting patiently for the murmuring and sounds of shifting bodies to subside. "The rules of witch trials are designed to be fair, as I shall explain and Monsieur Chassenée has misrepresented. Two or three witnesses testifying against an accused witch are sufficient to prove guilt. As to eligibility nearly anyone qualifies, and on this point the advocate and prosecutor agreed. Child may testify against parent, husband against wife, and vice versa. However, let me be clear about one point: *testimonies disputing the accusations are not permitted*—one serpent does not turn and bite another; a rook doesn't peck out the eye of its nestmate. Excommunicants, accomplices, outlaws, women of low morals, criminals, and drunkards were at one time disqualified until Pope Innocent VIII lowered the standard to ground level and washed his hands of the matter." Révigny suddenly threw both arms up as if praising the Lord and shouted, "Happily, nowadays anything goes!" The spectators, seeing the gesture as a cue cheered and clapped. "No accused witch is ever innocent!" They cheered and clapped louder.

"Monsieur, I was expecting a serious rebuttal presented in a positive light," said Institoris.

Révigny looked down at His Grace and gave the hint of a bow. "I'm nearly there, Your Grace." Returning his attention to the audience, he said, "Prior to trial an accused witch might be put to the rack as a means of clearing her mind of any confusion or doubt concerning guilt. Remember, guilt can't be declared without a confession, as the renowned Institoris himself has explained in this very room, but he was only mouthing the words. The law might so stipulate, but in actual practice such inconvenient impediments are swept aside in modern witch trials."

Raising his voice to a shout, Révigny said: "*Today, those who refuse to confess and subsequently bear up under the most intense torture, even to the point of having their limbs ripped from their bodies, are considered guilty by default, Satan having empowered them to withstand the pain.*" The room became still as Révigny paused in his oration for effect. Then in a softer tone, "Because our enlightened law forbids repeated torture, if a confession is not elicited the first day the judge may order it 'continued' the next day and again the next until the victim—pardon me, the accused—capitulates. In this way any later accusation of repetition, which would be a legal violation, is neatly avoided.

"But before 'continuing' torture on consecutive days the accused is shown the tools of pain and ordered, if innocent, to begin weeping at once. Witches, as everyone knows, are unable to weep, and if no tears flow she rightly may be declared guilty. If she weeps on cue the judge may order the bailiff to examine the tears to confirm they're genuine and not saliva or urine the defendant has surreptitiously splashed onto her face. Having been so assured the judge orders the victim released from the dock and led before him once again, although walking backward so he can see her before she turns and sees him, thereby protecting himself against enchantment and frivolous compassion. Her arms and legs might then be checked for the Devil's marks, although their absence is not in itself evidence of innocence."

Institoris had heard enough and interceded. "Monsieur Révigny appears to be leading us into the woods and fields instead of down a straight path with a clear view of the horizon. Like Monsieur Chassenée he too misses the objective. The Lord's orders are clear with respect to the fate of witches. In *The Book of Leviticus*, chapter twenty verse twenty-seven, we read: *A man also or a woman that hath a familiar spirit, or that is a wizard, shall surely be put to death: they shall stone them with stones; their blood shall be upon them.* A little redundant, perhaps, but certainly pointed. And in *The Book of Deuteronomy*, chapter eighteen verse ten: *There shall not be found among you any one that maketh his son or his daughter to pass through the fire, or that useth divination, or an observer of times, or an enchanter, or a witch.* And again, verse eleven of that chapter: *Or a charmer, or a consulter with familiar spirits, or a wizard, or a necromancer.* That seems to cover all possibilities, don't you think?" He leaned back in his chair, evidently satisfied the message had been received and perspective regained. From this relaxed position of authority he absently tapped his quill on the table and said to me, "Monsieur Chassenée, you may begin your defense."

CHAPITRE SEPT

THE THIRD DAY OF court, Wednesday the 24th of October, began cold and clear. Révigny and I, braced by several cups of hot tea and toasted loaves with jam, none of which we actually needed, walked briskly to the municipal building, collars upturned up and hands in pockets.

"Why does Ambrosine refer to you as 'Master' in discussions with me?"

Révigny shrugged. "Who knows? An attractive young witch. . .perhaps a term of respect for a decrepit old demon in the twilight of his eternal years."

His Grace nodded to me when the ringing of the bells indicating terce had stilled. I gathered my papers on the table and stood. "My friends," I said, "I begin my defense of Mademoiselle Ambrosine by questioning the nature of so-called witches and asking, what are they, really?"

Institoris intervened at once. "Monsieur, are you about to deny the existence of these beings? To do so, as you're well aware, is heresy."

"Not so much deny their existence, Your Grace, but investigate whether they can actually call forth and control the magical powers so universally attributed to them, such as ordering demons around, present the illusion of shape-shifting, and flying through the air. I accept that evil abounds, and that women and men with intent on doing harm to mankind lurk among us. Specifically, I shall open the defense of my client by questioning whether Mademoiselle Ambrosine or any other girl or woman accused of witchcraft is actually capable of *maleficium*, defined as the harming of another through the power of a demon. I shall argue that my client presently seated in the dock in plain view is just an ordinary country girl thinking nothing except girlish thoughts and without the intention of harming anyone.

"Do witches, necromancers, demons, or even Satan himself possess power over fleshly matter? This is both a deep philosophical question and one of immediate practical urgency to my client. In formal language, *qui formas convertere possit*; in the vernacular, can they change form? Man has power over himself. He can move his arms and legs, his mouth and eyelids, at will. However, he has such authority to control only his own body; it extends to no one else's. The question becomes, is it possible for beings with supernatural powers to manipulate such corporeal movements from outside a human body, perhaps even direct someone's thoughts? If so, and pertinent to the case before us, can they do this at the direction of witches? Keep in mind that a witch's powers rely on demons carrying out her orders. Oh, she may cast the spell, perhaps with the aid of special unguents, incantations, and powders, but— and here I must emphasize—*the spell alone is impotent, serving merely as a catalyst linking the conjurer with her desired result, an act performed by a willing demon.*" With these words I stopped pacing, jabbed a forefinger at the ceiling, and looked directly at the gallery.

"Pursuing the question along different lines, *must the demon obey if so ordered?* Presuming this issue and related ones—and I remind everyone than *père* Francisco de Toledo and other great minds are still pondering the matter—until settled and its elements distilled into canon, how can we not presume a simpler and more realistic probability that these so-called 'witches' are just harmless, delusional eccentrics? This surely would be the situation were we to acknowledge that regular women obviously lack supernatural powers of their own until learning to harness those extended to them by and through demons.

"And consider the likelihood of demons acting independently of witches, turning a deaf ear to their pleading for assistance but allowing them to believe they actually possess powers to order demons around. Demons, as we know, excel at deception. If either situation is true, what we call 'witchcraft' comprises only harmless rituals and senseless mutterings by corporeal, ordinary human females, those we greet each day as wives, sisters, daughters, friends, and neighbors. Their charms, unguents, and powders alone are ineffectual, and the evil we perceive is caused by demons acting under the Devil's orders, not these weak, gullible, and harmless women."

I pointed to Ambrosine. "In the absence of evidence to the contrary, that young lady in the dock must be exonerated at once, her place taken by a demon." I pounded my fist on the table and shouted, "*Surely, Satan and his demons bear guilt for the crimes of which she's accused!*" Boos and hisses assaulted me, along with rotten fruit and vegetables, bringing several scavenging pigs and two beggars running toward the court's main table to forage at our feet and the rooster to land directly on the table, gobble a morsel, and crow in triumph. *"Burn her! Burn her!"* the crowd chanted until Institoris rapped his mallet on the sounding block, then stood and raised his hand for silence.

Révigny now rose, imperious and impervious to the stinky missiles. Institoris, the clerk, and I were ducking and holding our arms in front of our faces, but nothing struck Révigny. Oddly, no one appeared to notice, perhaps being too occupied in the moment. When the ruckus abated Révigny said, "My friends, stay calm and open-minded. Mademoiselle Ambrosine has yet to be declared either guilty or innocent, so please withhold judgment. The questions and conclusions posed by Monsieur Chassenée are trivial. Remember, we have as our judge the peerless Institoris, author of the famed *Malleus maleficarum*, which is, we can state confidently and without disrespect to God or Church, the legal 'bible' throughout the civilized world for solving issues exactly like these. This noble work appeared on the 5th day of December, year of grace 1484 along with a bull of Pope Innocent VIII in which he declares that as guardian over the souls of all members of the Church the inquisitor Institoris is responsible for protecting us from heresy. Rest assured your souls are safe."

Révigny paused to pick up his notes. "The bull states, *But it is not without profound grief that I have learned recently that persons of both sexes, forgetting their own eternal welfare and erring from the Catholic faith, mix with devils, with* incubi *and* succubi, *and injure by witch-songs, conjurations, and other shameful practices, revelries, and crimes, the unborn children of women, the young of animals, the harvests of the fields, the grapes of the vineyards, and the fruit of the trees; that they also destroy, suffocate, and annihilate men, women, sheep and cattle, vineyards, orchards, meadows, and the like; visit men, women, cattle and other animals with internal and external pains and sickness; prevent men from procreation and women from conception and render them entirely unfit for their mutual duties, and cause them to recant, besides, with sacrilegious lips, the very faith which they have received in baptism.* Consequently, the pope appointed Heinrich Krämer as master inquisitor, granting him absolute power to find and stamp out these evils. Furthermore, there would be no appeals from his tribunals, not to other courts, not even to himself, to repeat words stated previously in this same room. His judgments would be final, and the pope exhorted him to carry out his mission with zeal, efficiency, and severity.

"In the *Malleus*, by which abbreviation we lawyers refer to it in admiration, the Great Inquisitor tells us that demons indeed receive the signals of witches beckoning them, either through incantations or by other means, and when receiving them know what to do. He provides an example in his glorious text. A witch desirous of causing a hailstorm. sticks her broom into a stream and after wetting it flings the end upward while still gripping the handle, allowing water to spray over her head. A demon alerted by Satan sees this, understands its meaning, and a hailstorm is soon on the way. From this and similar examples we know conclusively that witches not only are capable of summoning demons but directing them to carry out specific maleficent activities.

"And where does a witch obtain the formulations for her potions and unguents? From Satan's teachings. And the incantations and other signals to summon and direct demons? Obviously, from the same source! And as Arnaldo Albertini taught us, although demons are the principal instigators of *maleficia* these crimes are for legal reasons correctly attributable to witches. After all, how could the courts prosecute a demon or any supernatural being? It would be the same as putting air on trial.

"As for releasing the girl—mind you, a mere child—I must admit I'd rather get a real demon to stand in the dock in her place simply for the experience of prosecuting one, but sadly that isn't possible, at least in this substantial world. Think of it differently. Among charges against the accused is 'image magic': she made a wax image, proclaimed it to be a facsimile of her hated stepfather, and pierced it with pins. The poor man died the next day, bleeding from wounds over his whole body. Not surprisingly, a weapon wasn't found.

"Now, we can presume that the murderer was actually Satan. However, he had no motive to kill this man. The act was carried out by the girl in the dock mediated through the image she fashioned from wax. Can we prosecute Satan? Not directly, but we can prosecute *her*!" With this he dramatically extended his right arm and pointed at Ambrosine, who returned his look with an amused smile. "Our only choice is to proceed with what we have; that is, the substantial being before us in the flesh called Mademoiselle Ambrosine. Nothing could be clearer. The truth is, witches indeed walk among us, and they surely have the powers attributed to them." He sat down to a silent gallery.

My opening statement and Révigny's impromptu rebuttal had merged into a stalemate. Institoris, perceiving a natural break, adjourned court. Révigny and I gathered our papers and walked back to the inn. After depositing our belongings we also adjourned, to the tavern where the innkeeper jumped in response to Révigny's wave and promptly produced a flagon and two cups.

After seating ourselves comfortably and taking a sip or two I said, "I suppose Institoris will arrive in Hades a celebrity to be toasted heartily by members of Satan's inner circle."

"Then you would be wrong," Révigny said, to my surprise. "Nobody will be less popular in Hell than Henricus Institoris, taking into account the hundreds of witches he's burned, unwittingly delaying Satan's prospect of conquering Upper Earth for decades, maybe centuries. What a waste. Contrary to the reasoning of most, neither Satan nor his subterranean demons will rejoice when Institoris appears among us.

"Once when Institoris fell ill and thought death was closing in he tried faking remorse for having caused so many women to be burned, whether guilty or not. On realizing that Heaven wasn't even an outside chance, Satan responded with a pat on the back and told him, 'There's lots more witches where those came from. Just don't expect my help!' The meaning in this message was obvious, but Institoris didn't get it. Satan's often subtle bedside manner is greatly underappreciated. Institoris recovered, but Satan clearly implied that although the world can't ever run short of witches regardless of how many are torched, their effect is cumulative, and the input of each counts. From this Institoris should have deduced he would probably spend eternity in Purgatory, neither here nor there, fish nor fowl. Such a fate, if revealed to him now, would be terribly depressing and disappointing and surely result in many more putative witches being executed out of spite."

CHAPITRE HUIT

No sooner had court opened the next morning, Thursday October 25th, than Institoris himself stood to speak. A judge inserting himself into a trial this far along and elbowing aside the lawyers is unorthodox. The reason for the disruption in procedure, he explained, is that tribunals involving the occult must be conducted with proper background information entered into the official record, and being the world's foremost authority on witchcraft in all its manifestations he intended to provide this himself. Specifically, he would present an overview of witchly behaviors and practices not yet introduced and describe the nature of sabbaths so that everyone could gain an understanding and feeling for their evil.

The crowd quieted immediately on seeing him prepared to speak. "As is commonly known and already mentioned, women seem especially drawn to the practice of witchcraft. Having been charmed by Satan they relinquish themselves to him body and soul. What they receive in return is knowledge of demonic magic and the power for summoning demons to implement Satan's directions. Into their weak and tremulous souls seeps a warm feeling of being dominated by a power who recognizes and encourages their involvement. I refer, of course, to the Dark Prince himself.

"I warn the faithful to be ever vigilant against the insidious evil of women. They're born and die bearing the curse of Eve's guilt for the sin she committed in the Garden of Eden. Mankind would still enjoy immortality and carefree idleness were it not for Eve's meddling. We're told in the *Book of Ecclesiastics*, chapter twenty-five verse twenty-four, *Of the woman came the beginning of sin, and through her we all die.* Even the most righteous among them are tormented by carnal lust. And in the *Malleus maleficarum* I write: *What else is a woman but a foe to friendship, an unescapable punishment, a necessary evil, a natural temptation, a desirable calamity, a domestic danger, a delectable detriment, an evil of nature, painted with fair colors!*

"Women are easily seduced by illusions and false promises and eager to gain influence over others, particularly men. They gather in the night and ride on the backs of certain beasts, wolves in particular, in the company of the pagan goddess Diana. At such times their transvection covers great distances, drawing followers to infidelity, apostasy, and the general spreading of mischief and evil. I might add that the riding of wolves by witches on their way to sabbaths remains especially popular in Switzerland.

"Diana entered modern witchcraft through the canon *Episcopi*—literally, *Bishop*—assembled by Regino, former abbot of Prüm, and published in the year of grace 906. There for the first time she is implicated as giving humans animal shapes. The *Episcopi* warned bishops and the clerics under them to beware of *maleficium*'s harmful magic, advising them to stamp it out whenever and wherever the vile practice appears and to severely punish its adherents. The Church has no tolerance of superstitions. In his *Decretum*, in the vernacular *The Decree*, Burchard de Worms in the 11th century repeated the text of *Episcopi* twice, stating that witches could travel in the company of either Diana or Herodias. Leader of the Night Ride was identified as Holda. He accused such a woman, *while still in your body, to go out through closed doors and travel through the spaces of the world, together with others who are similarly deceived; and that without visible weapons, you kill people who have been baptized and redeemed by Christ's blood, and together cook and devour their flesh. . . .*

"Women like Holda, called *strigae*, were believed to kill men by consuming them from the inside. This ungodly predilection put early witches in a category with the pagan *lamiae*, hags who slay children at night while they sleep or utter curses that leave them crippled and diseased. To some believers the *strigae* sacrifice children to *lamiae*, cutting them into small pieces before eating them. The pieces later are vomited up, and if the Devil expresses pity they are reassembled and returned to their cradles. From children the *strigae* carry off and submit to ritual murder they sometimes eat the fat.

"Witches are known to leave their marriage beds and unsuspecting husbands in the night and travel to a sabbath, the location of which was known only to them. How can they vanish without their husbands knowing? There are several possibilities. Satan might have slipped the husband a soporific causing him to sleep so soundly as to be unaware of his wife's absence. If the husband later testifies that his wife had been with him through the night it could be argued that Satan had deceived him into thinking this by substituting a demon in the form of his wife, or perhaps bewitching the man into believing the being beside him is actually her.

"Sabbaths usually take place on a Thursday or Sunday. Not until the 12th century was the true evil of *maleficium* recognized, and in its early days witchcraft was punished far too lightly, practitioners sometimes being exonerated with orders to do penance when today they are righteously prosecuted, convicted of their crimes, and burned.

"To become a practicing witch with any real power often comes at terrible cost. Satan frequently demands collateral from the living to secure his loyalty and backing, and these aren't mere tokens. It often means pledging limbs to him after death or offering their children to be sacrificed and eaten at sabbaths. Stories are rampant about witches sucking children's blood and consuming their flesh at sabbaths. The flesh of babies tastes like young pork. It has a sweet flavor, and when properly cooked becomes so tender as to fall spontaneously from the bone. Some have claimed that following these feasts the bones are dried and made into diabolical powders and unguents, sometimes mixed with night soil procured from a Jewish quarter, the ultimate degradation. Were that not gruesome enough, such concoctions might variously include the hair of animals and Jews, threads from altar cloths, or dead mice.

"From Spain comes Pierre de Lancre's description of a sabbath in which witches perform night flights to cure the sick, a rare exemplum of altruism, although the potions and unguents retain their same gristly or-igins. Supposedly, they prepare themselves according to certain secret rituals before taking to the air like a flock of birds accompanied by their toad dressed in human clothing. When effecting a cure they repeat these words: *emen hetan*, *emen hetan*. It means 'here and there, here and there.'

"The more powerful witches—those who have promised to Satan anything he asks—can bewitch the weather by calling up hail, thunder and lightning, blizzards, even avalanches. They can induce drought by bewitching the rain to stay away. By scattering powder made from murdered children and the bodies of snakes and scorpions over the landscape in a mist, the land is rendered forever sterile. The same can be achieved by filling a cat skin with grain, soaking it in a spring for three days, drying and pulverizing the skin and its contents, and dispersing its dust into the wind from a mountaintop. Any land touched is sterile from then on.

"Witches can fly through the air, inure themselves to pain on the rack, take over a judge's mind by making him feel compassion or sexual longing, change them-selves or others into animals, enchant and kill men and animals by their look. Their one true addiction is to the taste of the flesh of baptized babies, which they devour to satiation at sabbath feasts, although unbap-tized children make nearly suitable substitutes if not quite so tender and often described by witches at trial as having a 'gamy' aftertaste. Think levitation is impos-sible? Remember, Satan carried Jesus to the pinnacle of the temple. It's right there in *The Book of Matthew*, chapter four verse five: *Then the devil taketh him up into the holy city, and setteth him on a pinnacle of the temple.*"

I noticed that Institoris had avoided looking at Ambrosine, but he did so suddenly and pointed directly at her. "There, good people, sits evil incarnate. Don't be fooled by her false appearance of youth, innocence, and beauty. Just beneath that skin lurks a monster, Satan's acolyte and sex partner, one who cavorts with demons and savors the tender flesh of baptized children." If this maneuver was meant to frighten or intimidate her it failed. She looked at Institoris with a steady gaze, inducing his to fall.

Institoris, maybe hoping to regain the upper hand, began an intense interrogation. He raised his voice and looked at her sternly. "Do you own a book containing instructions for summoning the Devil and casting evil spells on others?"

"Of course."

"Which volume?"

"The *Grand Albert*."

Institoris dropped abruptly into his chair, appearing stunned. In a voice that now sounded uncertain, he said, "That book is beyond rare and nearly priceless. Where did you obtain it?"

"That's none of your business."

"Very well, if you insist on being difficult."

"I do."

"Clearly. Are you able to read it?"

"Of course not. Are you?"

"I don't like your impudence, mademoiselle."

"The problem is entirely yours. I don't like anything at all about you, in particular your arrogance and your lustful stares. Don't expect me to kneel at your feet with clasped hands and closed eyes and say two Paters, two Glorias, and two Aves. Instead, you should kneel at *my* feet and renounce your crassness, stupidity, and hypocrisy."

The room was now nearly silent, the air barely trembling on a low current of murmurs. The accusation of lust directed at the Great Inquisitor had fallen with the impact of a meteor. Institoris seemed paralyzed. He picked up his papers distractedly and put them down again, stalling, wondering what to say and do next, but the damage had been effected; Institoris had suddenly become the *de facto* defendant. Ambrosine had knocked him back on his heels and swung the rabble to her side. The murmuring stopped. The foraging animals stood still as statues, and they too looked at the dock. The only sound was of wind wriggling softly through open chinks in the stone walls.

Institoris stood again, smoothed his robe, and continued his monologue as if the interruption had never happened. "From the earliest days of Christianity the issue of demons conjoining with witches in despicable carnal acts has been discussed by ecclesiastics, the learned philosophers of many lands, and even some saints. Many theories were proposed over the centuries, often polluted and rendered illogical by myths and superstitions of the times. In these times we must acknowledge that such abominable behaviors practiced from the beginning of mankind's appearance on Earth remain with us. Perhaps such urges and tendencies are ineradicable features ingrained in our humanity, destined to infect us until the end of time. Sadly, we seem unable to excise and expel from our souls the foul tumor of Original Sin. The poof is irrefutable. Mankind's vulnerability to bewitchment has been passed down to us through woman starting with Eve's temptation in the Garden of Eden.

"Demons, like humans, are of two sexes, the male equivalent being an *incubus*, its female counterpart a *succubus*. In ancient times *incubi* commonly infested unwilling women by raping them, as Johann Nider has written in his marvelous treatise, *Formicarius*. But that, as the saying goes, was then. The modern era is vastly different. Today's *incubi* have little inclination to pursue chaste women because so many who are unclean willingly embrace their foul advances, gladly accepting a life of heresy and filthy servitude while fully understanding that the cost is eternal damnation.

"For those who still doubt this occurs and that demons and witches walk among us, don't take my word alone or the words of ecclesiastics, other learned men, and saints. Merely look to the law and many recorded confessions of witches whose verity must be considered both expert and credible despite its disgusting nature and origin. Ponder how they acquire this grotesque addiction to evil, often as girls of only twelve or so years. Think how demons induced them into unspeakable acts of carnal sex, even orgies, and heretical behaviors such as treading crosses underfoot and spitting on consecrated wafers. To further bolster the truth of what they confess to the inquisitors consider that many spoke following severe torture, nonetheless knowing they were destined for fiery deaths at the stake. Surely, they would not have admitted to such frightful charges had their own words not been spoken truthfully before God.

"My *Malleus maleficarum* is deeply concerned—some critics say obsessed—with how copulation between witches and demons is actually accomplished. It poses four questions in this regard. First, what part of a demon's body is used in fornication? This might sound odd, but demons can alter their limbs and phalanges to suit any purpose. In other words, we can't simply assume an *incubus* has a sexual member, much less uses it to penetrate the vaginas of witches, but if so does this organ resemble an ordinary man's? Second, is coitus always accompanied by ejaculation of semen obtained from another human male or do demons on occasion favor birth control and practice *coitus interruptus*? Perhaps a witch who wants to avoid pregnancy uses the proven methods of regular women, like tying the uterus of a barren bitch to herself or exposing her pudendum to smoke from a burning mule's hoof. Third, is copulation engaged in more often at one time than another? And fourth, is coitus between a demon and a human visible to an ordinary person nearby?

"A matter long debated and of crucial ecclesiastical importance is whether the sexual act between a demon with a witch always results in the injection of semen. Demons, of course, don't produce semen. Although Satan has infinite ways of undermining the Church, an ability to increase the population of its adversaries would certainly be to his advantage. The condition of the witch at the time of copulation is undoubtedly important. To produce offspring she must still be of reproductive age and not a shriveled crone, in which case the semen is wasted. But we know that *incubi* are nonselective in their sexual desires, and witches of all ages are considered desirable and only rarely rejected. Sex, therefore, isn't always about procreation as the Church mandates.

"As to the women, is being conceived in this manner a requirement to becoming a witch or were they offered to Satan by evil midwives at their births? Could they perhaps have been recruited by established witches under whose tutelage they train as apprentices? We find in the record frequent cases of witchcraft being handed down through lineages from mother to daughter. In some instances girls of just three and four years are being taught the black arts by their mothers and aunts, learning the rudiments of boiling toads alive, killing and eviscerating rats, and fashioning likenesses of despised persons then injecting them with pins. It's no surprise that such girls grow up eager to fornicate with demons and even animals they acquire as familiars. After all, the commonality of witches and sexual laxity has been known for centuries. Finally, is the venereal delight greater or less than coitus with a mortal man? Suppose we find out by asking an actual witch? What do you say?" Institoris raised both arms and gazed over the crowd.

They responded: "*Yes! Ask her! Ask the witch!*"

Ambrosine stood and turned to face her detractors, and her words, spoken in that disarming little-girl voice, charmed and shocked them to silence. They sat mute, as if bewitched. "Demons have members covered in bumps, making sex with them far more delectable than with mortal men, who have only smooth penises. We witches call these unusual members 'French ticklers.' Many say demons have airy members, but they sure feel stiff to us witches."

Institoris had evidently been hoping to intimidate Ambrosine in some way, maybe inducing her to weep or plead for mercy, anything except admitting in a clear, calm voice that she was indeed a witch. He sat down heavily and slumped in his chair. Convicting her would be considerably more difficult if she succeeded fully in captivating the public. The defense attorney and prosecutor already had belittled and tarnished his reputation. The thought occurred that he was no longer invincible. I glanced at Révigny and saw his eyes flashing bright red, which Ambrose also noticed and gave him a pleasant smile. Institoris, unable to perceive this exchange between insubstantial beings and feeling out of sorts, adjourned court.

Later, as we relaxed in the tavern, Révigny said, "Institoris is a noted pervert and voyeur. Satan truly hates him, as I've said already, although not for these qualities, which he generally finds admirable. We've monitored his antics for years. During one notable inquisition Institoris expressed unusual fascination with two women accused by three men of 'binding' their members with small, invisible stakes and rendering them unable to have sex. We speculated whether his own member has been bewitched and reduced to a state of permanent limpness. His blatant obsession is collecting information on the possible mechanics of how women copulate with demons, often standing nearby when a woman accused of witchcraft is put to the rack so he can hear and record any details. Admitting to fornication with these beings is inadequate to satisfy his curiosity. He wants to know specifically how, why, when, where, and the exact mechanisms of penetration and ejaculation. When listening to tales of demon sex he gazes at the accused with a half-smile and dreamy expression, as if mentally masturbating.

"Demons fashion temporary bodies out of materials gathered from air, but only theologians still question whether such beings can eat, drink, digest, excrete, and indulge in sex. Ha! Being a demon myself I can state with certainty that the answer to the first two processes is yes, to the next two, no, and sex? Absolutely! I assure you, our sexy little witch in the dock knows too from firsthand experience.

"Regardless of the form a demon assumes we can be certain it isn't the corporeal kind but rather inspissated, which I shall explain. Air, as everyone knows, takes no form but rather modifies its shape to fit the space enclosing it. Air is also invisible. During storms when vision is limited the cause isn't the air itself but elements incorporated from the sky, water, and ground. Condensed water we know as fog, or mist. Sometimes visibility can also be rendered opaque by terrestrial particles, dust stirred by breezes and made airborne. However, we can be certain that the air carrying them—pure air—still remains invisible.

"Think a moment of the shape of water, which presents much the same dilemma. An ancient proverb from Cathay says that if the bowl be square the water contained in it will be square too. In this way we have demonstrated that air must be forced into a mold of some sort to have shape, and this is exactly how demons are able to be seen. The air used by a demon so it can appear visible to humans must be inspissated, or congealed, in the shape of the human or creature infested. We can thus ascertain that visible demons consist of congealed air together with other aerial particles conveniently acquired; in other words, the 'mold' of which I spoke that holds the imprisoned air in the demon's desired form. By this means demons can, like the air of a storm, turn opaque and become apparent to varying extents by gathering terrestrial particles and vapor condensed from the atmosphere, just as bricks can be shaped from powdered clay mixed with water and poured into a mold. However, if the air used is pure then the demon remains invisible to the human eye.

"Because a demon is composed solely of congealed air, piercing one using a sword, dagger, pike or any other sharpened weapon is impossible. The object will simply pass through leaving the cleaved portions to instantly reassemble; a hole poked in its fabric closes without leaving a scar in the identical way you've watched my cocoon anneal after being punctured. A demon is capable of taking any shape and once formed can swim, walk, fly, run, or move by whatever means it chooses. Angels can too, which is perfectly logical considering that demons are simply misbehaving angels."

Révigny stretched out his foot. We watched as the big toe grew suddenly to enormous size and appeared to acquire a life independent of the other toes. "You see? This sort of entertainment would never be permitted in Heaven. It's so, well, undignified. God and Jesus would frown at such frivolity.

"Anyway, the source of the semen remains a mystery both to serious theologians and dedicated perverts like Institoris. Here are the facts. As a being consisting of congealed air a demon is incapable of producing its own semen and must obtain it from a living man, preferably one of low morals and diabolical tendencies. Human children often acquire the traits of their parents, so it seems reasonable that a demon in search of semen would avoid a righteous man of good standing in his community and shadow an evil derelict instead. The demon might steal his semen by catching it during a nocturnal emission, or by inserting his hand into the mouth of the wife's vagina and at the instant of ejaculation capture the emission undetected. By whichever method he then carries it away to inject later into a willing witch through his own airy, compressible member.

"Today's science claims that a woman plays no part in conception and gestation, her womb serving merely as a source of nutrients for the fetus and a convenient means of conveyance. Thus, the modern view of reproduction holds that a woman already pregnant by her husband can become doubly so if a demon injects her with the semen of another. The child she delivers will be a composite of two men, one of them infected with sperm tainted by the hand of a demon.

"Of secondary and more practical concern to Institoris is the nature of powders and unguents prepared from the bones and fat of babies both baptized and unbaptized and details of their formulations. When the discussion shifts to pharmaceuticals he turns serious and studious, frantically scribbling notes. Institoris is often the main subject on the agenda of our weekly roundtable discussions down below. It's interesting how so obvious a deviant and misfit could rise to the very top of the inquisitorial profession. Some in our group have postulated that his true interest might be opening an apothecary. There's certainly profit to be gained in compounding and selling diabolical products of standard composition and proven efficacy. And there's no shortage of babies to supply the principal raw materials."

At that moment our supper arrived, the usual barely edible fare served at inns throughout France: a few soggy vegetables and pieces of greasy meat floating in a broth decocted from soupbones. It was accompanied by two small loaves. We didn't much care, considering that demons and ghosts don't experience hunger and thirst. We taste and swallow, but don't digest and excrete. If the food is too foul we push it aside and go without, ordering more wine to fill the time. I sleep fitfully, Révigny not at all, which makes sharing a bed convenient. He simply disappears for the night, off to observe or participate in whatever mischief amuses him, then meets me for breakfast the next morning.

Chapitre neuf

We come now to Friday, October 26th. Prior to the opening of court His Grace summoned Révigny and me to a vacant corner of the room where we huddled and conversed in whispers. He admonished us to pay closer attention to our duties, specifically as they affected the Church's objective. By this he meant prosecuting a known witch efficiently and without undue controversy. He emphasized his displeasure with Révigny, accusing him of not vigorously pursuing what clearly was an open-shut case. It seemed to him almost as if the prosecution and defense were in collusion in siding with the defendant.

He was right, of course. Révigny and I long ago concluded that those in the dock, whether rats, pigs, werewolves, or witches are so rarely exonerated that their trials seem farcical, little different from theater where the outcome is preordained and fools no one. And we, two of the court's principal members, are present merely to act out our parts. The rules—call them the set pieces—had been arranged with such bias that neither side could, in the end, be said to either "win" or "lose." In truth the legal system wins; the defendant not only loses but pays the price. For opposing lawyers the rewards are monetary and a chance to gain fame. In the end the exercise is a zero-sum game, gains and losses of one side balanced by those of his opponent. Neither can actually come out on top. As I was musing about the so-called matters at stake and listening with only one ear, Institoris not so subtly instructed Révigny and me to go forthwith before our waiting audience and step properly into our roles. The trial, he said, should have ended by now. Taking more than three days to try and convict a witch was unheard of, certainly in trials he judged. Another two or three of similar duration, and he would be a laughing-stock among his peers. Had we been serfs or oxen he undoubtedly would have scourged us for lassitude.

When the bells stopped ringing Révigny stood. Holding a fold of his robe in each hand, he said, "Good people and Your Grace, my objective this morning is to determine the limits of the defendant's witchy powers. Not every witch is the same, as some you know and the rest suspect. Every defendant is different, and her degree of accomplishment and prowess must be ascertained to determine innocence or degree of guilt." At this, Institoris raised his eyebrows and looked up at Révigny as if to remind him to get on with it, that the outcome was predestined. Révigny appeared not to notice the gesture and said, "Naturally, a young girl apprenticed to an experienced crone is certain to be less accomplished than her mentor. Thus, her powers and the damage she can cause are lessened accordingly."

Révigny shifted his gaze from the audience to my client. "Mademoiselle Ambrosine, are you related to a crone now deceased known locally in your home town of Bourgon as Auntie Ambrosine?"

"Yes, monsieur. She was my grandaunt, my grandmother's sister."

"And was she burned alive for the crime of witchcraft after confessing to carnal actions with some of her familiars, namely a dog, a cat, and a rooster? These familiars were demons, of course."

"Yes, monsieur."

"And did she not also admit during her trial to having been a practicing witch for many years?"

"Yes, of course. Auntie took me in as a young girl to be her apprentice."

"I understand you are presently fifteen years of age, or thereabouts. How old were you at the start of your apprenticeship?"

"I was around ten years, monsieur. Auntie was burned when I was thirteen, or thereabouts."

"So, you were an apprentice witch for two years and have been on your own for three?"

"That's correct, monsieur, but I missed out on much without Auntie's tutelage. You can learn a lot by attending sabbaths. There's nothing like being personally mentored night and day. Casting spells is all in the details."

"How were you enticed into this despicable life of sin and corruption? Did Satan promise to sate your greed and vanity? Did he offer you wealth, beauty, eternal youth, and other earthly advantages and delights?"

"He didn't promise anything. I appear young because I am, and my appearance has always been my own. Do I look wealthy, sitting here barefoot in a ragged tunic?"

Révigny leaned against one wall of the dock and propped an elbow on the railing. "I see your point, dear girl. On a related subject, what can you tell me about the science and art of necromancy?"

"I've only heard the word used, but never knew what it meant."

"Then I shall explain because it's possible that you are not only a witch but a necromancer as well, in which case your punishment could be even more severe. Necromancers are quite advanced in the realm of the occult."

Ambrosine looked at him innocently, eyes wide. "You mean they could burn me twice?" This elicited low murmuring and a scattering of uneasy laughter from the spectators.

Révigny himself chuckled. He lifted his elbow from the railing and stood erect. "Necromancy, a close kin to witchcraft, involves summoning and conversing with the dead for purposes of predicting the future. The practice is undeniably demonic because a demon serves as the medium. Nothing much happens unless a necromancer can summon an appropriate demon and establish rapprochement. Here the philosophy becomes tenuous. Saint Augustine points out in his treatise *De divinatione daemonum*, in the vernacular *On the Divination of Demons*, that evil spirits including demons lack true prophetic knowledge and therefore can't predict the future. They can, however, proclaim suppositions based on their exceptional perception, speed in moving about rapidly, and extensive knowledge and experience of human frailties. The resultant conjectures are transmitted falsely to people as divinations. So, we must ask ourselves, is necromancy viable or simply a ruse?

"Whichever the case we know it to be almost exclusively a masculine endeavor. Why? Because the texts used as guides are complex and often written in foreign languages; few women possess sufficient education to interpret them. By default a successful necromancer is a scholar of considerable erudition. Are you a scholar, mademoiselle?"

"Hardly, monsieur. I was never taught to read, write, or compute numbers."

"Can you write your name?"

"Yes, but beyond that I have no formal learning."

"Insofar as the Church is concerned a necromancer can only be in league with Satan. However, as an illiterate female you could scarcely qualify to join such an elite body of intellectuals."

"I suppose not, if membership requires reading, writing, and number skills."

"May I assume you consider yourself as simply a witch and nothing else?

"That's right."

"A witch who has served only a portion of her apprenticeship."

"Yes. Auntie had much left to teach me."

Révigny stepped away from the dock and faced the spectators. "Let's discuss the difference between magic and miracles. I've consulted the writings of two of our sainted Christian theologians on the subject and will keep it brief. Saint Augustine of Hippo, born in the 4th century of our Lord, wrote that all magic is real and without exception demonic. Saint Thomas Aquinas, writing in the 13th century, agreed, adding that only God can perform miracles, never demons or humans.

The phenomena demons occasionally produce are therefore real, although never miraculous. He cites as an example Pharaoh's magicians producing real snakes and frogs. He also agreed with Saint Augustine that transformation of humans into animals is impossible. Do you agree with the writings of these great figures of history?"

"I can't read, remember?"

"But I just told you their words. Don't you believe me?"

"I don't believe anyone. I believe only what I can see, hear, feel, touch, and smell. Nothing else."

"Very wise. Can you change yourself into an animal?"

"Of course not."

"Can you fly through the air?"

"Naturally. I'm a witch."

"Are you able to perform miracles, such as raising the dead?"

"No. But I can cause mischief that to some might be seen as miraculous."

Révigny once again approached the dock and leaned against it. "In the town of Ratisbon an unwed young man had an ill-advised sexual encounter with an unmarried young woman and afterward lost his member. When examining where this part once had been he found only smooth skin. Would you define what happened as miracle or magic, and could you duplicate such a feat?"

"It's magic. The man was enchanted after having sex with a witch. I could duplicate her feat given the right unguents, powders, or required incantations. The witch cast a spell on the man after having sex with him, a spell only she could reverse."

"Tell me, mademoiselle, have you ever practiced midwifery? I ask because midwives are more wicked by far than other women. They do more than deliver babies; as healers they routinely handle powders and unguents, items often associated with witchcraft and Satanic rituals."

"No, monsieur. I've never liked babies unless boiled or turned on the spit." This brought a mixed reaction from the gallery, some viewers shocked into spontaneous gasps or curses, others breaking into raucous hoots and laughter. A drunken man who approached the dock and attempted to pour wine on the defendant's head was quickly clubbed to the ground by the bailiff's men and dragged unconscious out the door.

When the ruckus dissipated Révigny said, "Witches have been considered a threat even to popes. In the year of grace 1320 Pope John XXII ordered his inquisitors to include all forms of sorcery in their investigations. Why? Because he was afraid his enemies would use magic against him! Tell me, mademoiselle, are you sufficiently powerful to enchant a pope?"

"No, monsieur. Doubtfully even a *curé*. The pope exists in a realm protected by its own magic, well outside my power to do him harm. Of evil beings, probably just Satan himself could pose a threat, and it could be only with God's permission."

"I shall now turn to the subject of womanhood in general and after my disquisition will ask your opinion on certain aspects. Do you understand, mademoiselle?"

"Yes, monsieur, I think so."

"Good," Révigny said, turning to face the crowd, most of whom were certainly destined *not* to understand. "The Church has always felt threatened by marginal beings, and by these I mean Jews, gypsies, animals. . .and women. The *Malleus maleficarum* is a hateful polemic on the female sex." At this, Institoris began to twirl his quill, a scowl on his face. Seemingly unaware of the gravity of this remark, but actually not caring, Révigny continued, and Institoris kept silent.

"The *Malleus* lies, claiming, for instance, that Jesus advised men not to marry and quotes *The Book of Matthew*, chapter nineteen verse ten. Jesus actually didn't say this. He was discussing something entirely unrelated, namely, adultery as reason for divorce. The *Malleus* then accepts Jesus at his word while justifying divorce anyway as a means of ending relentless suffering: *Therefore if it be a sin to divorce her when she ought to be kept, it is indeed a necessary torture; for either we commit adultery by divorcing her, or we must endure daily strife.* In other words, divorce indeed alleviates the daily suffering, the pain and anguish of an existence defined as Hell on Earth. To suffer now or in the afterlife is the decision to be faced, made easier if the current life with an unpleasant woman seems an eternity.

"Solomon—the exemplum of mankind whose wisdom is considered unsurpassed—had been tempted by the feminine sex, to his great regret. Another wise man, Saint John Chrysostom, wrote: *What is woman but an enemy of friendship, an unavoidable punishment, a necessary evil, a natural temptation, a desirable affliction, a constantly flowing source of tears, a wicked work of nature covered with a shining varnish?*

"Eve entered into a pact with Satan, who appeared to her in the form of a serpent in the Garden of Eden and tempted her with the forbidden fruit of knowledge. She accepted, resulting in the expulsion not just of herself but Adam too. They went abruptly from ease and eternal life to God's sentence of toil, pain, anguish, and eventual death. Their descendants continue to suffer the consequences of Eve's astonishing betrayal of God and her husband. I scarcely need remind you that the word *femina*, or woman, refers to one deficient in faith; *fe*, of course, means 'faith,' and *minus* is 'less.'

"Having been formed from a crooked rib, woman's spiritual being has always been warped, tending more toward sin than virtue, toward darkness than light. As Seneca wrote, *Woman either loves or hates; there is no third possibility*. Following this logic we can deduce that a woman who doesn't love God has no choice except to hate Him. Therefore, understanding why women are so enamored of witchcraft is easy. And consider that woman is even more evil than Satan. How so? Because Satan fell only once, from his incarnation as Lucifer, and in his failings Christ the Redeemer did not suffer on his behalf. Satan's sins are only against God the Creator, but the witch? She sins against both Creator and Redeemer. There can be no mistaking her malicious intent.

"Now, mademoiselle, do you believe that being female relegates you to the category of marginal beings?"

"Definitely, monsieur. Women everywhere are disrespected and devalued for their many important contributions."

"Do you believe that divorce is a form of adultery,

and if married and cast out by your husband would you leave willingly?"

"I would never be so stupid as marry, monsieur. The question is without meaning to me." The audience found this amusing and responded with delighted catcalls.

"Do you believe that a woman who professes not to love God can only hate Him? Do you hate God?"

"I can't speak to what other women believe. As to God, I neither love nor hate Him. Truthfully, I don't think about Him much at all." This response gave the spectators a chance to hiss and direct curses her way.

Révigny now paused, then turned to face His Grace and me seated at the main table. He raised his right arm and pointed a finger as if at the sky and said, "And what, mademoiselle, is your opinion of the great work known as the *Malleus maleficarum*? I must ask to know where you truly stand." The room seemed to inhale and hold its breath. In the charged silence even the rooster stopped clucking and scratching at the earthen floor.

"In my opinion, monsieur, it's a collection of lies, hatred, and horseshit. A pig has more dignity, grace, and compassion than its author, who himself should be tied to a stake and set alight, as surely he will be in Hell."

Then the room exhaled, a massive sigh sounding and smelling of fear and confusion. Institoris jumped to his feet, nearly knocking me out of my chair. "That's enough!" he shouted. *"Monsieur Révigny, I hold you in contempt! Bailiff, take him to jail at once! Court is adjourned until Monday!*

Chapitre dix

THE THREE OF US sat on the pallet in Ambrosine's cell. It was afternoon, a bit after nones as indicated by the weak remnants of daylight leaking through the high window. I asked Révigny why he did it, purposely go so far afield and abandoning his duty as prosecutor by showing sympathy to the defendant and blatantly embarrassing a judge so powerful as Institoris. What could possibly have been his motive?

"Think a moment, Barthélemy. It was the pompous bishop of Paris who damned me to hell originally on my deathbed when I told him the truth, that he was a liar and a pederast. I hated such authority figures in life, and death hasn't changed that opinion. Satan is different. He has a sense of humor, and he's suffered what for a being like him must certainly be the ultimate degradation, being tossed out of Heaven. Even Satan has felt humiliation. But Institoris? He needs to pay his dues if he wants to be seen as a truly evil person with status. His political stature must be reduced, then we can see if he's capable of rebuilding it. The next several days are going to be interesting. Anyway, the three of us are well beyond any sort of earthly punishment, so why worry?

"I believe we're missing the entire point of this trial,

which is to have fun. To this end humor me while I review the rudiments of theater and interject a few of my own experiences in this regard. Barthélemy knows the basics of acting and stage-setting, but he hasn't yet heard my stories." He turned to Ambrosine, who was leaning against him, her other shoulder against the wall. "And you, dear girl?"

"I'd like to learn about these things, Master," she said.

Révigny cleared his throat of brimstone smoke, coughed once, and began to orate. "The means by which novice poets and playwrights are taught to construct dramatic truth is *inventio*, a mental space where violence and poetics merge. In drama *inventio* creates and establishes illusions of truth; *memoria* then commits them to memory and rehearses them. Actors often recall their cues by the use of mnemonic devices. Typically, successive speeches are linked by octosyllabic rhyming couplets. For example, *Gestas, Gestas, tu as grant tort/ Tu te dampnez sanz nul ressort*. Subsequentially, *actio* enacts them through the protean mechanisms of delivery. If delivery isn't believable the sequence collapses. Through these three means are an actor's lines remembered and delivered to the audience along with appropriate voice inflections and body language, the elements of 'drama,' or 'the dramatic.'

"Be proud, *mes amis!* Hold your heads high! We're in the company of Homer and Turold! Remember, Plato said that lawyers are as much illusionists as poets, that 'we are composers of the same things as yourselves, rivals of yours as artists and actors of the fairest drama.' Our lawyerly duty is to fuse emotion and truth so tightly as to make them indistinguishable. And what is 'truth,' you ask? Whatever we predetermine it to be.

"As rhetoricians our objective is to persuade with the ultimate goal of convincing. And persuasion, once *inventio* and *memoria* have been planted successfully in the audience's mind, derives from *actio* implemented in the oral delivery and body language, the latter including gestures of the face, torso, and limbs. An actor's mien determines how the audience perceives his performance and encompasses all these, in addition to dress and everything augmented by the stage set and illumination. Their sum can produce, for example, a humorous mien; alternatively, one that's foolish, serious, or noble.

"Since ancient times it's been established that the performative mode of rhetorical discourse is manifested in *actio* and the actor's capacity to signify: breath control, voice modulation and tone, body movement. . .whatever is required to make the audience tremble fearfully, writhe with uncertainty, laugh uncontrollably, or weep with the greatest sorrow. The best actors are masters of eliciting these emotions in others. Acting is mimesis, and we're actors. You too, mademoiselle, because the defendant is on prominent display throughout a trial and makes her own contribution to the overall performance. Especially in this proceeding, considering we three are in league to promote the conservation of witches. No matter which side of the law Monsieur Chassenée and I represent—or appear to— we're acting out our roles on a stage before an audience comprising a judge and the people.

"In court Barthélemy and I employ what could be

called 'forensic rhetoric'; that is, enactment of judicial proceedings with actual results that have meaning and consequences, as opposed to purely dramatic rhetoric in which everything is a game of representation. Keep in mind that the person on trial faces life or death. The proceeding might be entertainment and nothing more to the audience, but defendants, those of substance and actually capable of losing their lives, view it differently. For this reason Thomas Basin advocated eliminating the entire oral presentation from our French legal system in a futile attempt to separate the law from performance. Naturally, he failed. Why would lawyers ever want to relinquish the stage?"

Révigny now lifted his chin and turned his eyes upward, a dramatic gesture of his own I recognized. It indicated reprising a fond memory. "Satan and I saw a play in Seurre, a reenactment of *Mystère de Saint Martin*. I believe that was in the year of grace 1496. A mishap of some sort occurred during the performance when the clothes of the actor playing Satan's role caught fire and badly burned his ass. Satan laughed so hard he doubled over and actually shed tears of boiling brine. Nobody except Satan can do this. I saw the liquid evaporate on his face leaving a deposit of salt underneath each eye. As it turned out the poor actor was seriously injured, news that delighted the Dark Prince even more. He promised to swear on a Bible he hadn't been responsible, but who could vouch for the sincerity of that oath?" This drew a tinkling laugh from Ambrosine. Révigny smiled, displaying his green teeth and gums and ostentatiously slid out his forked tongue.

"Even earlier, in 1437, an actor taking the role of

Judas was hanged on stage and nearly suffocated. He was quickly cut down and vinegar held to his nose to revive his heart, which had stopped.

"Satan and I missed that play but caught another even better, the famous performance of *Laureolus* when condemned criminals were actually tied to stakes and burned alive. Let me just say, an audience will readily abandon a theater in the middle of a lively act on receiving word of an imminent execution nearby; the latter is by far the more 'theatrical' spectacle, by which I mean entertaining, because the violence is guaranteed to be real. The fascination of observing death is unmatched.

"And when you combine a play with an execution?" Révigny pushed his green fingertips of one hand together and kissed them as if praising a splendid vintage or exquisitely prepared *pot-au-feu*. "At the end of *Laureolus* the delighted audience called out the actors for three successive ovations. There they stood, bowing and throwing kisses, backed by smoldering corpses. The evening had been windless, and the odor of crispy human flesh hung in the air long after the play-goers departed. It was a performance for the ages." He looked at me. "Have you ever visited the site of a burning the next day?"

The thought was revolting. "No," I said. "How disgusting."

"Disgusting? Barthélemy, you surprise me! A man of such epicurean tastes as yourself should seek all possible knowledge, even of the unpleasant genre. How can wisdom spring from the flames of knowledge—pardon the queasy metaphor—if all sides of an issue aren't examined carefully and without bias?

"Well," he said with feigned disappointment, "if you ever do poke around such a place you'll be astonished at the amount of grease left on the ground. A typical human contains as much fat as a pig of the same weight. When burnings are conducted on bare earth the grease remaining is food for rats and cockroaches, which come surreptitiously in the night to feast on it. But a burning carried out on a stage finished with flagstones leaves a permanent stain that can never be washed away, even with lye. The town's dogs, cats, and vermin then spend hours attempting to lick it up, but that which has soaked into the rock stays for years. And, I hasten to add, makes the stage dangerously slippery for actors in future plays. You could say it's Revenge of the Torches! These spectacles are always such a delight to eye, ear, and nose.

"Remember the modern theatrical dictum, *Il faut du sang*? And so, blood there will be! What can be bloodier and more spectacular than a public execution? In modern times the most famous execution ever folded within a play was a drama featuring the biblical Judith and Assyrian general Holofernes. It was staged at Tournai. This was the ultimate in staged violence. You know the story, of course. Nabuchodonosor, king of Babylon, sends General Holofernes and his army to subdue the Jews by putting the city of Bethulia under siege. Throughout the ordeal the people trapped inside the walls are languishing and losing hope. Then Judith, a widow, and her loyal maid begin sneaking into the enemy camp at night and gradually befriending Holofernes by offering him information about the status of the besieged residents. One night when Holofernes gets drunk in his tent and passes out, Judith cuts off his head and returns with it to Bethulia. The distraught Assyrians, their leader having been slain, break the siege and retreat.

"Directors of the play, anticipating royalty to attend in the person of Prince Philip II, devised a twist sure to please a monarch renowned for his cruelty. They decided to substitute a criminal for the character of Holofernes. The man had been convicted of heresy and several murders and was to have his skin peeled away with red-hot pliers prior to being burned alive. When told of his proposed role he readily agreed to its terms, wishing at all costs to avoid torture and simply be executed.

"At a critical juncture in the drama a strong young man dressed in women's clothes was to be secretly substituted for the actress playing Judith. In the shadows he really would behead Holofernes, or rather his stand-in. And so at the crucial moment as he pretended to sleep, 'Judith' grabbed 'Holofernes' by the hair and sliced off his head with a scimitar. Blood spurted from the victim's torso as the severed head rolled away, and the body gave several violent death spasms, releasing a sanguinary shower on those closest to the stage. The response of the audience spanned outrage to enchantment. Some shouted curses of damnation while others clapped and cheered. According to reports, children fell dead on the spot and pregnant women aborted spontaneously. People vomited from disgust and horror with equal spontaneity, or simply fled screaming from the scene, some later to go mad. Prince Philip was heard to remark, *bien frappé*. Well struck, indeed!

"There are many similar stories, although not quite so grisly. I could tell of plays I've seen in which penitents actually volunteered to be nailed to crosses and even had their sides pierced to emulate Christ's passion. A piercing of the side can be fatal if administered too enthusiastically. No matter when it's a slave who's nailed to the cross. He isn't a trained actor, of course, and has no lines, no *memoria*. If he dies or is rendered useless the play's director simply pays the owner an amount agreed to beforehand in case of such accidents.

"The earliest of these dramas were liturgical. Later, they were called *passion* plays, and today we refer to them as *mystères*. They've been around so long that enactments have become difficult to distinguish from reality. Of course, actors and the roles they perform are real too, just not always representative of what's experienced in daily living where truth can become lie and vice versa. Clever *mise en scène* and superb acting can veil even the subtlest reality. Nowadays, any receptive audience arrives filled with latent fear, ready to be stampeded like frightened sheep by the most blatant falsehood. The event awaits only the moment of bloodshed.

"In another play Satan and I attended the slave on the cross couldn't speak a word of French. Then Satan, standing in the audience embodied as a young nobleman, gave him voice. 'You don't believe I'm the chosen one, the Child of God?' he thundered, then added in words layered in self-pity and rectitude: 'You sons of bitches, stick your hand in my wound! *Do it!*' The man's side was pierced suddenly by an invisible sword. Blood flowed, and he fainted. *Il faut du sang!* The director, suspecting demonic interference, kept his head as if nothing unusual had happened and afterward enjoyed the huzzahs of the audience. But the performance had astonished. People cheered, wept, fled, or fell to their knees praying fervently and clutching their beads. It was hilarious. Satan and I dropped to the ground convulsed in laughter, both of us choking inside our personal clouds of brimstone. 'God-*damn!*' Satan shouted between violent coughs, in words only I could hear.

"That play had some interesting consequences for the cast. A couple of members later killed themselves, one entered the priesthood, and still another succumbed to despair. The priest who administered last rites declared that 'despair killed him as he despaired.' If such a conclusion seems ridiculously tautologous the law contains many similar examples. I once prosecuted a vampire. At his sentencing the bailiff read that the criminal was 'to be executed until death,' which I suppose covered all possibilities.

"I end these little remembrances by pointing out that executioners and actors are the only professional guilds denied civil status, making them legal and social outcasts in modern French society. Why? Because both perform acts that alter the human body, executioners through torture and sanctioned murder, actors by assuming postures and mannerisms stolen from the characters they mimic. In ecclesiastical terms, only God has authority to transform the human body. Also, because man was made in God's image only God has the power to transform his shape. To believe otherwise is heresy. Members of both guilds are respected while performing, but the audience is always edgy, waiting for a moment to degrade them. If an execution is botched or an actor forgets his lines the crowd might erupt, insulting him and driving him away. Executioners and actors are pariahs except when nestled within their specific coteries.

CHAPITRE ONZE

On Monday morning October 29th I continued my defense. "My client is an admitted witch. Nonetheless, I continue to argue that based on ignorance of youth she should be given another chance at a normal life. Some in the gallery have already convicted her in their minds and can barely wait to see the kindling ignited at her feet. They and others like them think my attempt to have Mademoiselle Ambrosine exonerated is more difficult than changing the positions of the stars or making pigs fly. Actually, Monsieur Révigny has the harder task: he intends to argue with certitude that God not only is Catholic, he's French." Révigny chuckled; Institoris scowled but held his tongue. "Just a little joke to see if everyone is awake," I said.

I left my chair and went to stand in front of the table where my short stature would be completely visible to the gallery. "In legal terms Mademoiselle Ambrosine, although an acknowledged witch, is innocent of her accused crimes by having been under decision-making age when introduced to witchcraft. She's still a mere girl today. It's my legal contention and sincere personal belief that the witchy forces exerted by her grandaunt exceeded her undeveloped psyche's capacity to ignore and overcome. Try as she might the tug of an experienced witch proved too compelling. Children are always at the mercy of adults, moreso when the adult possesses supernatural powers. Then there is the added force of Satan himself whose call none except the rare few can resist, and only then through direct intervention by one of God's angels." I pointed to a man standing in the front row. "Could you ignore Satan's powers, monsieur?" He shifted uneasily. I pointed to a middle-aged woman wearing a coif. "And you, madame, standing here before God and your fellow man—tell us, could you defy Satan if he cast his fiery eyes on you and beckoned?" She looked away, avoiding my gaze. "I thought so," I said. "Anyone here who this very moment can swear before God the irrefutable capacity to repel Satan's entreaties, raise a hand." I scanned the room, as did everyone else. "I don't see a single hand. Not even my own.

"Many gathered in this room have surely acquired at least some of the wisdom that comes with age. I can see the potential in your lined faces and bent backs, your gnarled hands. You have persisted through hard times, learned from those experiences, and survived. If even the wisest can't summon sufficient courage to resist the Devil under any circumstances, no matter how trying, how could a girl of fifteen years be expected to repel his advances, an evil being whose power is second only to God's? Is that reasonable? Is it fair? My client can no more conquer the urge to murder and devour babies than a cat can resist killing and feasting on mice, a dog can refrain from chewing a bone, a hungry cow willingly ignores a lush patch of clover." My voice rose to a shout: "*Mademoiselle Ambrosine is the victim in this case, not the perpetrator!* She's merely a poor young soul whose impulses are controlled by the Evil Prince! These so-called accusations, even if true, aren't her fault. Who among us could be blamed for falling under Satan's influence? Remember, it isn't always voluntary. The Devil knows every spell and enchantment, the formula of every potion, unguent, and powder. He's a master alchemist. Think of the saints and the suffering they endured for their love of Christ. Worshipping Satan requires the same emotional investment, but directed toward darkness instead of light.

"And consider this: even if you deplore witchcraft and believe all witches ought to be hunted down and eradicated, the punishment Mademoiselle Ambrosine faces if convicted is barbaric. The morals of insensate lions and tigers are superior to those of the inquisitional courts. Anyone knows that dumb beasts commit no crime by killing other animals for food. We kill them for food too, don't we?" I shouted, *"Burning human beings alive is cruel, inhumane, and purposeless!"* I bowed my head sadly, adding that I couldn't imagine a more painful death, especially when inflicted on a defendant still wrapped in the innocence of youth's naïve bliss. I clasped my hands as if in prayer and pleaded that the convicted should be strangled by the executioner before being burned regardless of age.

"These are trying times, beset as we are by demons all around, ruled by a clergy that sets itself on a higher plane than the rest of humanity and propounds a mission to chastise instead of cherish; hounded by plagues of all sorts, invisible scourges that stalk us persistently while recognizing no hierarchy, whether man's or God's."

Institoris stopped twirling his quill and looked up. "Be careful, Monsieur Chassenée. Heresy is knocking at your door once more. I dare you to open it."

"Yes, Your Grace," I said as I returned to my chair.

Révigny rose. "May I rebut, Your Grace?"

"By all means, Monsieur Révigny," Institoris said. "I very much look forward to hearing a rational presentation. Please bring us back to reality."

Révigny nodded and stood. "My colleague's compassion is admirable. As to who is and isn't resistant to Satan's song I couldn't say. Historically, the courts have extended leniency to those too young and innocent to make decisions without adult guidance, although at age fifteen a girl is almost a woman, if not one already. Many are married and have borne children at younger ages. That, however, is neither here nor there. More serious is my adversary having forgotten that pain is part of the punishment in capital crimes.

"He also forgets or ignores the crucial fact that a person having been invaded by a demon relinquishes every vestige of her earthly being. Her screams are no more expressions of anguish than those emitted by an unreasoning beast at slaughter. Animals experience pain in the nerves, but their dim minds are unable to make sense of it. As lower creatures they have no way of placing their feelings in context. A cat emits a noise if swung by its tail, but can we be certain the noise is a yowl of pain or merely surprise? When we burn a witch we ignite a demon's repository, once a human form but now a shell devoid of its previous humanity.

"Fire is the only proven method by which demons can actually be destroyed. Once the fire has been lit we must remember too that the object tied to the stake is merely a vile sack stuffed with evil, reduced to a vessel in which to cook the demon it sequesters. As to this defendant being an adolescent, remember that no one is legally exempt from punishment because of age, whether old, young, or in between. I once saw a baby of three months burned with its mother, the latter a convicted witch, the baby guilty only of having displayed an 'evil eye' to several witnesses. Some can *donner le mal*. You heard me correctly: cast a spell simply by a glance. The result is to make the victim *sécher*. In the vernacular of some parts of the country this means to die slowly and painfully. For obvious reasons never look a stranger in the eye. I have nothing further, Your Grace," said Révigny. "This concludes the prosecution's case."

I stood and said, "The defense rests too, Your Grace."

"Very well," said Institoris. "The defendant will now rise and hear the verdict. Bailiff, take your place beside the dock."

Before sitting I paused momentarily to examine my documents, which were increasingly difficult to read. The atmosphere was changing, taking on a sinister feeling. The ambient light had dimmed without my noticing, and I could barely make out the letters in front of me. Today had dawned with a scowl, and by sext its mood had turned decidedly fouler. The municipal building where we held court had been constructed so crudely, the stones cut, set, and mortared so carelessly, that on such days the wind whistled through and having gained entrance complained like softly jabbering demons. The tip of its tongue was palpable. It licked around the corners and crept sinuously along the dirt floor, tickling the ankles of the crowd and alerting the snouts of scavenging pigs and dogs. Every human, beast, and fowl stirred uneasily. A constant undertone of mutterings and muted snuffles and whines pervaded, the atmosphere now settling ominously like gray ash. Even Institoris seemed uneasy, his eyes darting here and there, quill twirling nervously. The room had grown suddenly cold and smelled of exhaled breath, stale clothing, and barnyards. Then abruptly the light faded nearly to darkness as if presaging a storm. Institoris called for the candles in the wall sconces to be lit, and we sat in silence while the bailiff's men scrambled to carry out his order.

No sooner did the candle flames rise than a single gust rose from the floor and blew them out leaving the dock strangely brighter than the rest of the room, as if illuminated within or cast under a strange aura. Still, no one spoke, but all eyes turned to Ambrosine whose hair looked more golden except better groomed: combed, coiffed, and lightly powdered, and in it was a tiara of sparkling diamonds. Her face was a picture of perfect symmetry, the cheeks rosy; her blue eyes were even larger, their pupils assuming greater depth and mystery. Adorning her was a gown of exquisite silk the color of her eyes, trimmed in ermine and purple velvet, the bodice displaying a promising cleavage. Her feet were encased in satin slippers fit for a royal ball. Then she vanished abruptly leaving a donkey in her place. It now wore the gown and the tiara between its ears, and it was grinning. The crowd, which had inched closer to view the astonishing spectacle of this other-worldly woman gasped and stumbled back. I knew immediately what was afoot.

"Your Grace, a moment, please." I stood to full height, clicked my heels together, and attempted to button the flaps of my jacket across my stomach, a futile undertaking. "Despite the many times dumb animals and even *bestioles* have been put on trial I know of no instance in the law even hinting that an earthly creature of any kind, whether beast, fowl, or insect, can be summoned before a judge, secular or ecclesiastical. I refer, of course, to the ass in the docket. I therefore ask to be shown written legal precedent, and if none can be produced then I insist my client be absolved of all charges and released at once."

Institoris' response was immediate and astonished: "Who is this woman. . . this *thing*? Bring the prisoner from her cell!"

"But this *is* the prisoner, your Grace," said the bailiff, who had been holding Ambrosine's elbow. "She was just standing here." He looked at the donkey and then his hand, maybe expecting it to hold a lead.

Révigny let out a guffaw followed by a violent coughing fit as smoldering brimstone inside his cocoon filled his spectral lungs.

I ignored the distraction and said, "In the year of grace 425, Augustine of Hippo wrote in *De civitate dei*. . . . " At this moment Institoris looked at me sternly. Anticipating a rebuke I corrected myself. "Pardon me, *City of God* in the vernacular. Anyway, according to Saint Augustine demons can through enchantment assume the appearance of beautiful celestial angels to susceptible persons of unclean souls. We must examine such beings carefully when they appear to us, knowing a mortal human is incapable of such transformations. What we actually see is a demon taunting us, an evil illusion from which we must look away. Those who violate this admonition have unclean souls because the apparition is visible only to them. As we know today more than a millennium after Saint Augustine's warning, to participate in rituals involving these beings is apostasy, and those guilty are heretics, slayers of the celestial soul. Sitting in judgment of this trial is to join in such a ritual. I can't testify to the cleanliness of His Grace's soul nor what his eyes tell him he sees, but my own reveal only my client, Mademoiselle Ambrosine, sitting in humble impoverishment in the witness chair."

Institoris became furious, his face contorting with rage. "*How dare you call my soul unclean!*" He was shouting and pounding his fist on the table. Just then the donkey brayed and stamped a hoof.

I placed my hand on my heart in a gesture of innocence and said calmly, "Not at all, Your Grace. You implied this yourself. I was speaking only in generalities. You alone know if your soul is defective. Any disagreement over the matter is between yourself and God." Institoris took his eyes off the donkey and glanced at the spectators, evidently to assess how they were responding, and in that instant the donkey disappeared and Ambrosine stood in its place, smiling benignly, still dressed like royalty.

I badly needed a red herring to divert and quell His Grace's fury. I said, "As Your Grace knows only too well, animals can sometimes be evil. I myself have defended a sow that devoured a baby in its bassinette, and such events are more common than most think. Sometimes the evil is inborn, at other times acquired. In the matter of this vision that evidently appeared to you miraculously, who can say which was the origin? Monsieur Rodet, the renowned French veterinarian, reported that in every cavalry regiment is at least one horse refusing to be controlled and if not restrained will readily attack its companion horses and even men. Such an animal can be identified by its narrow forehead and down-turned muzzle. Rodet called dangerous horses with these distinguishing skull malformations horses with a hooked nose; in his exact words, *chevaux à nez busqué.*

"And we've long known about Herr Büchner's 'thieving bees' too lazy to perform the labor of ordinary bees. They instead attack the hives of industrious neighbors, kill the residents, and steal their honey. It seems that such acts aren't learned, but organically stowed and arise from within. But are they always heritable and thus predictable traits only in certain lineages of bees, or can mitigating factors induce the same or similar traits? Whether beasts, *bestioles,* or men, we might be quick to call such beings 'born criminals' had not Büchner reproduced this exact phenomenon in normal bees by mixing brandy with the honey they drank. Soon his treated bees became indolent and irritable, giving up foraging for themselves and when becoming hungry attacking unaffected hives, murdering the inhabitants, and carrying off their stores."

Institoris had suddenly become calm. "All quite illuminating, Monsieur Chassenée, but I have no idea what you're talking about. This has no relevance to the proceeding. Please stay on point."

Meanwhile, Ambrosine had taken her seat in the

dock, again shoeless and wearing her tattered tunic, apparently having enchanted Institoris and everyone else in the room. Time for them had passed unremembered. In their amnesic state her appearances first as a princess and then a donkey never happened.

I sat musing. Saint Augustine's interpretation of time seems obvious and mundane, yet fabulous. If nothing *passed* there could not be a past, and history would not have been. If nothing *happened* there would be no future time. And if nothing *is*, present time could not exist. People ask, how many years make up eternity? Monks have gone insane pondering the issue. But years are arbitrary human inventions, calculations based on the movements of heavenly bodies, the changing of seasons. Eternity has no breaks or pauses, no stops and instants of acceleration, no beginning, middle, or end. In eternity, time doesn't exist.

In general, we understand that time is a component of the material world because we measure it solely in earthly contexts. Time began at God's command. In the *Book of Genesis*, chapter one verses fourteen to nineteen, we learn that the Last Day will come when He wills it. That moment will coincide with Christ's second coming, the instant earthly time collapses into eternity. Living humans are subject to material time, explaining why life is transient. In contrast, existence in Heaven and Hell is timeless and thus perpetual. Infinity extends forever. Ambrosine, as if reading my thoughts, gave me an impish smile of a sort only Révigny and I could perceive. Excepting a few enchanted beings, such signals, as I was learning, fall outside the purview of the living.

That morning on our way to court Révigny and I had passed a dead mule in the street. Such sights are common, and we thought nothing of it. The beast had died in harness. Several men, including its owner, were attempting with difficulty to salvage the ropes and leathers, parts of which were pinned underneath the carcass. Our thoughts were currently on the matter at hand: Institoris was about to pronounce judgment on my client. The sudden breeze that earlier had blown out the candles seemed to have lessened. The bailiff's men had lit them again, and the flames were now standing obediently upright instead of guttering to extinction. The air of the room was again turning stale.

A ruckus outside suddenly drew everyone's attention. People were shouting and screaming, seemingly in terror. A deep booming sound was causing the air pressure inside the room to rise and fall rhythmically, as if alternately sucked in and expelled by gigantic bellows. And then the candles went dead again. The room began to empty as spectators pushed through the door to see what was causing the disturbance. Institoris ordered the bailiff to investigate and report back at once. Révigny's eyes were flashing red, and when I looked at Ambrosine she gave me an impish smile and mouthed the words 'Monsieur Tonnerer,' which meant nothing to me, although Révigny's evil grin signaled that it did to him.

The three of us followed the crowd outside leaving Institoris behind, and the sight we saw was marvelous beyond imagination. In the street stood a hunched vulture easily the size of a dragon and stinking of death and decay. It was biting huge bloody chunks of flesh from the dead mule, tilting back its head, and swallowing them with loud gulps. Each chunk was the size of a small pig. The spectators, although clearly terrified, were too fascinated to turn away. And what, exactly, were they seeing? The carcass of a large mule shaken like a rag with each beakful, these savage movements accompanied by the wet sounds of flesh being wrenched from bones and swallowed. An entire mule was shrinking before their eyes in enormous bites. However, the entity causing this havoc was invisible to all but Ambrosine, Révigny, and me. "That's my vulture," said Ambrosine matter-of-factly. "I call him Monsieur Tonnerer because when he lands it's with a loud crash and rumble causing the ground to quake. He has this habit of beating his wings while eating, disturbing the air pressure all around, causing the 'thunder' to persist and popping everyone's ears."

"He's Mademoiselle Ambrosine's familiar," Révigny explained.

"That's right," she said. "He's my ride when I need to get to a sabbath. He's impressive but comes with a downside. There's the stink, of course. And his breath! And being a vulture he insists on landing whenever he spies a carcass, which is why I'm always late. Monsieur Tonnerer was a stupid vulture in life, and even now hasn't realized that as an outsized demon the hunger he feels never can be sated no matter how many dead animals he eats. He's actually pretty disgusting, but I've grown fond of him and still keep him around."

By the time court had returned to normal the verdict was almost an afterthought. Naturally, my client was convicted of witchcraft and declared a heretic, her sentence to be burned alive. The bailiff was to summon the executioner, gather kindling, and erect a stake in the square of the Avaricum district. The event would take place at terce a week hence, November 5th. Meanwhile, Institoris himself would be relaxing at his vast estate outside the city. The bailiff could send a messenger in event of an emergency.

Chapitre Douze

Institoris no sooner arrived at his grand manor than Ambrosine, from her jail cell, proved her prowess as a *meneur de nuage*, and to label her someone who could call forth a storm would be a wild understatement. Had it been summer she would have instructed her army of demons and familiars to raise a fierce wind to flatten Institoris' fields of ripening grain then carve them into vast geometric circles, but the year was growing late. Instead, she summoned a hailstorm that destroyed his extensive crop of winter wheat just poking through the ground. As if to flaunt her power she remained seated on the pallet in her cell, eyes closed as if dreaming, declining to ride the clouds and direct her minions. Her skill was such that she could complete the task using force of mind alone.

Immediately before this event the bells of Cathédrale Saint-Étienne de Bourges began tolling spontaneously, startling the idle bell ringers who were lounging inside the belfry drinking tea and awaiting the hour of sext before pulling the ropes.

Institoris, having been called by his foremen to examine the wheat fields, immediately suspected witchcraft. He dispatched a messenger to ask Ambrosine if she had been responsible for this catastrophe. The messenger returned with word from Ambrosine advising his master to check his granaries, that she had just sent a pestilential mold to infect them. True to her prediction, within one cycle of the sun all his vast stores were destroyed by the fungus and overrun with rodents, the grain not fit even for livestock or poultry feed.

Institoris ordered the bailiff to put Ambrosine on the rack at once and continue torture until she agreed to reverse the damage and not initiate further attacks on his properties. The bailiff went to the jail immediately, intent on carrying out his assignment, but the cell was empty. The crippled jailer claimed she had been there just a moment before. He was accused of lying and enabling a witch and put to the rack in her place, but despite excruciating pain to his already deteriorating joints held fast to his story. When he was at last released and returned to his duties he discovered that the stretching had actually helped. His joints were now limber and pain-free, and he no longer limped.

While Institoris was bewailing his losses Ambrosine conjured an early frost that burned his vineyards, causing the late grape harvest to fall to the ground. On that same day the head vintner reported that the estate's fine vintages for which it was famous throughout France—hundreds of barrels aging in massive cellars—had turned to vinegar. Shortly afterward the estate's herd of nearly a thousand swine went mad, ignoring the panicked swineherds and breaking through the fences protecting the vineyards. There they devoured the fallen grapes and those remaining attached as high as they could reach before trampling the vines themselves into the mud and destroying them. Of the fields and vineyards, nothing viable remained.

The orchards fared no better. A sudden infestation of worms ruined the year's apple, pear, and peach harvests, leaving the fruits to rot on the ground unfit for market, although the cattle and swine enjoyed them immensely. Apples make cows flatulent, as every farmer knows, and soon the fields stank of swamp gas.

The fruit had no sooner dropped when Ambrosine announced by messenger that Institoris could expect an explosion of tent-worms come spring, blanketing these same trees and consuming every green leaf until his orchards resembled a winter scene when the limbs lie bare and dormant. As Institoris wept, another message advised checking his cattle because she had infected the entire herd with a plague. Every cow and calf, every bull, was destined to sicken and die within three weeks; meanwhile, the bewitched cows in his dairy barns began yielding blood instead of milk.

The swine now grown fat and prosperous were suddenly measled down to the last piglet. Of the survivors none would be marketable. The onion crop still in the field had withered. The hens stopped laying; the geese and ducks had lost their down and would die of cold with the first snowfall. The carcasses of all these unfortunate beasts and fowl would decay in the pens, coops, stockades, and pastures, palatable only to vultures, foxes, crows, and other scavengers. Institoris was ruined.

The final insult occurred the morning of Ambrosine's scheduled execution. She had returned periodically to her cell, often enough to bewitch the bailiff and jailer into thinking she had been imprisoned there all along. But on the morning of November 5th while the stake awaited and the crowd was gathering to watch her burn and hear her shrieks, she lifted all previous enchantments and escaped her cell in the guise of a mouse. As a joke she ate some of the jail swill before disappearing through a crack in the wall.

By then Révigny and I were well away from Bourges and bound for, well, somewhere. I had dispatched François and Alvin back to my estate with a message to Madame Chassenée that I was on assignment for a new trial in a different part of France and would send word with details eventually. Not that she would care or even notice my absence. Jamet was with me and now riding the palfrey. Révigny had presented me with a magnificent demon horse. It had a coat of gold and fire in its eyes. Could it fly? It could do anything. He was lecturing now, filling me in on the nature of demons, necessary information considering I was about to become one myself.

"Consider, Barthélemy, that if I present to you as an *i*llusion then your perception of me as real is a *de*lusion. Some demons never need to change form. They do so only to distract and confuse humans. Others, like basilisks and cockatrices, always look like what they are because human fear gives them all the power they need. But creatures living in the deep sea are monsters that never change, and they glow greenly from ports on their sides and often their eyes and backs too. Of all his creations God cares the most about humans and how he can punish us for Original Sin. He frankly doesn't give a shit about unthinking beings swimming through perpetual darkness. Why should he?

"I went to London once, sailing to Dover from Calais. That was when I was still alive, of course. The ship left at sunset. That night while leaning over the railing I saw an astonishing sight. As the bow cleaved the swells the water glowed green, which quickly subsided with the ship's passing, as if a curtain had been pulled over the face of the sea. The green glow slipped along the sides of the vessel bright enough to briefly illuminate the moonless night. The source comprised uncountable miniature demons flashing their lights, angry at our disturbance. I didn't know this at the time, nor did the sailors, but they had a name for the phenomenon, something to do with phosphorus. As alchemists know, phosphorus gives off a greenish glow.

"The fireflies you see flashing on summer nights? Many are demons in disguise that for unknown reasons enjoy copulating with actual fireflies." He paused. "I can extend you the power to see all demons. It's the skill both demons and witches possess. As a witch I knew once put it, she could 'pick out the devils dressed in their fancy clothes'; she could 'see' the true Others as they cavort or merely pass through our earthly world. You have only to ask. However, as you might suspect, there's a certain cost." He smiled wickedly, and I felt a shiver pass along my spine.

"Humbert," I said, "be honest. Are you Satan?"

"Assume that if I'm not Satan I'm at least his trusted adviser, his personal lawyer you might say. . . . "

I interrupted with, "That isn't an answer, that's lawyer talk."

"Right, but legal training is useful anywhere, and in Hell especially. You'll find yourself with lots of clients, most of them, like you, having wallowed gleefully in all the deadly sins. Your avarice is commendable. You cheated even the treasured clients who trusted you as friend and confidant. Everyone down there is always negotiating for better conditions and requires representation. The most common request is for a personal fire that burns cooler, but that's only one issue. The reading light is truly terrible, as I've mentioned before. And concentration is nearly impossible with thousands of demons running around shrieking and banging metal objects, the screaming of the damned, the crackling of a million fires, and all that noise ricocheting off the cold, dreary stone.

"And for all but the inner circle the wine is truly bad, worse even than Purgatory's. I can't even describe the pissy green swill in that place where the rules are even more relaxed, and consider this: if you were once a nobleman and now stuck there, you must fetch it yourself. Only a select few are allowed to bring their servants. Trust me, eternity in Purgatory seems twice as long if you're standing in line for a refill, forced to listen to the inane gossip and general bullshit from your fellow sufferers delivered in whiny voices."

"You describe this as if you had a vote in who is admitted into Hell and who stays in Purgatory."

"So it seems. Well, don't take me too literally. I'm simply another inmate." He grinned, and his face disappeared abruptly behind the brilliant red flash of his eyes. My trial experience told me I'd struck a nerve, and that Révigny was abjuring.

He quickly changed the subject. "Remember after the werewolf trial at Magny-Cours when I returned to Autun? There was mischief waiting there, including a little task especially dedicated to Madame Chassenée, bane of your earthly existence and as close as any substantial human can resemble a witch in habit and appearance. Without actually joining a coven, that is. She badgered and berated you into buying an expensive coach with two prime coach horses delivered from Paris by a coachman named Aufrey, who became a permanent member of the household. She then spent most of her days galivanting around the countryside visiting friends and putting up at their estates, all the while belittling your physical stature and mannerisms."

"All true," I said ruefully. Mention of my wife elicited only painful memories. "And when that machine gave out from excessive use I bought her another in the hope she might stop badgering me."

"Well, I planned a surprise for her," said Révigny. "Aufrey has been stealing from you even before he arrived. Those 'repairs' to the first coach on the road from Paris? He paid the shop owner a few sous and got a receipt for many more, which he put in his pocket after you repaid him for traveling expenses. He's quite accomplished at skulduggery. As proof, he got away with it right under the nose of so masterly a cheat as yourself, and to think how you trusted him implicitly. Therefore, you owe Aufrey no favors either. In fact, Madame Chassenée knew he was embezzling your funds and extorting the tradesmen of Autun and didn't tell you. They conspired in keeping you blissfully uninformed.

"Anyway, the event I planned happened November 1th shortly after Mademoiselle Ambrosine's trial. That was a Thursday, All Saints' Day, when the people were celebrating in their best attire intending to waste the rest of the week and the weekend. At Autun it's quite a festival. Those few owning coaches were parading ostentatiously through the streets, Madame Chassenée among them. At the moment of sext, as she and Aufrey were passing Cathédrale Saint-Lazare d'Autune, I bewitched the hundreds of bystanders. All subsequently witnessed your coach transformed instantaneously into a pumpkin, your sleek, prancing coach horses into mangy hedgehogs in miniature harnesses. Everyone and everything associated with the coach became visible in proportion. Inside sat a tiny Madame Chassenée, although not as she had imagined herself in the previous moment. The coachman? He appeared as a monkey still wearing his cap and tailored uniform with epaulettes. The pumpkin skidded slowly past Autun's high society, finally stopping directly in front of the bishop himself waiting to cross the street, showering his white tunic made of the finest silk from Cathay with mud and manure. And there sat Madame Chassenée and Aufrey, she in her phlegm-stained nightgown and wearing her nightcap with the point like the bent beak of a chicken, Aufrey jabbering in confusion and smelling of horse piss and moldering fruit."

I was stunned. Unable to think of something intelligent and relevant, I said, "Why a pumpkin?"

"Why not?" said Révigny. "A pumpkin is a useful vegetable, and I simply thought it appropriate under the circumstances. Centuries from now children will hollow out pumpkins and carve faces of demons into them. They will place candles inside. From doorsteps all along dark streets these faux demons, eyes glowing with orange fire, will illuminate the night."

"And Madame and Aufrey, what happened to them?"

"They became themselves, of course! After the

crowd swallowed its amazement and had a good laugh, and after the bishop berated your wife and coachman and all but damned them to hell, they returned to just what they were, although I allowed the memory of the event to stay with everyone who saw it. The story will pass down through generations."

Révigny started to laugh, and his laugh infected me. We both laughed as if only laughter mattered, we howled and guffawed and held our sides as if the Universe would suddenly falter if we stopped. "I'm sorry, Barthélemy," said Révigny when he finally stopped wheezing, "but I'm again shedding tears of boiling brine. Oh my!" He clapped a hand over his mouth in the mock gesture of someone accidentally spilling a secret.

And then I knew. Oh, I knew, but I didn't care. Suddenly, I was handsome and muscular as a Grecian god with golden hair to rival the hide of my demonic steed. Brimstone smoke wafted over me, and I inhaled it like the purest air. I needed it to breathe as a fish needs water, a worm its viscous mud. "What's next?" I managed to gasp.

"Anything, my friend. We shall oppose each other in court for eternity. What could be more scintillating than prosecuting and defending the despicable, the horrible, and the merely awful? Now mount your fine steed and ride."

And ride it I did. I galloped on the wind, and overhead I heard the thunderous wingbeats of Monsieur Tonnerer. He was tracking us from above while scanning the landscape for rotting carcasses, Mademoiselle Ambrosine astride his feathered back.